To Richard and Hellen

Into my heart an air that kills
From yon far country blows:
What are those blue remembered hills,
What spires, what farms are those?

That is the land of lost content,
I see it shining plain,
The happy highways where I went
And cannot come again.

A.E. Housman.

PROLOGUE

The Jaguar XJ6 bore down on the traffic island at a heart-stopping seventy-five miles an hour. The big man at the wheel gritted his teeth and began doing elaborate things very quickly with the gearstick, foot pedals and handbrake. Somehow he managed to slow the machine sufficiently to drag it screaming around the obstacle in its path, only clipping the kerb fractionally on the far side. The manoeuvre was a triumph of willpower over the laws of motion and friction, and there was a grin of achievement on his face as he accelerated away again.

At his side Malcolm Sheppard cursed under his breath; he hated it when the Chief insisted on driving. A police driver would have got them there just as quickly, if not more so, and without hurling him around in his seat and excoriating millimetres of tread from the expensive Michelins at every change of direction. But Kenneth Hamilton fancied himself as an expert at the wheel and it would be a brave or foolish Superintendent who tried to tell him otherwise. Malcolm Sheppard was not foolish, and preferred to save his bravery for those situations that deserved it, and which would advance his career rather than stop it in its tracks.

Seven minutes of this chaotic progress later, they were being saluted past the road block. Hamilton pulled to a halt at the end of an untidy jumble of cars, vans and motorbikes - most of them marked police vehicles - and a single fire tender.

They climbed out and made their way across to the knot of men and women clustered outside the mobile incident room. The crowd parted to let them through, and at the centre a hard looking man, with iron grey hair and eyes that did not blink, greeted them.

"Hello Ken. Good of you to come." There was neither warmth nor gratitude in his voice.

"An armed siege on my patch? I'm hardly going to stay away." He scowled at the television camera crew nearby. "I see the fourth estate is here. Who told them?"

"I've no idea. They arrived almost as soon as we did."

"Okay. So what's going on?"

Robert Taylor pointed to the large, Victorian house across the road, which was the centre of all the attention. "They're in there, and they've taken one of my men hostage."

"How many?"

"Don't know. Two went in, but others could have been inside already."

"Do you know who they are?"

"The man they've taken, Neil Lamb, had infiltrated a group calling themselves the Popular Front for the Liberation of Planet Earth. Bunch of environmentalist cranks. They've let off five bombs in as many months. Lamb was just beginning to get somewhere. They must have rumbled him."

Hamilton nodded. Life under Commander Robert Taylor of the anti-terrorist squad was a risky business. "What had he found out?"

"That's the curse of it - he was deep under cover. We hadn't heard from him for a month, and he was trying to report in when they caught him. Must have been following him. He's not told us a thing."

At that point there was a shout from one of the marksmen training telescopic sights on the house opposite. All eyes turned to see the distant view of a man, his back towards them with his hands tied behind him, framed in an upstairs window.

"Don't shoot," Taylor shouted needlessly. Hand-picked, highly trained police marksmen do not discharge their weapons just because something moves in their line of sight. Taylor trained his binoculars on the man opposite.

"It's Lamb. They're telling us he's alive. And using him as a shield. If they start shooting, we'll just have to duck - we can't return fire with him there."

Malcolm Sheppard had acquired a pair of binoculars for himself, and was focussing them on the window. "Things must be pretty tense in there. I've never actually seen anyone wringing their hands before."

"Let's see." Hamilton put out his hand and his Superintendent passed him the glasses. He watched for a couple of seconds, then, still grasping the binoculars, he bounded away towards the television crew who had been banished beyond the plastic tape which marked out the police command zone. Barging his officers aside he leapt the tape and grabbed a cameraman roughly by the arm. Waving wildly towards the

6

window he shouted at the startled man: "The hands. Film the hands. And don't stop - if you run out of film I'll eat you!"

Puzzled but unquestioning the man hefted his camera onto his shoulder, zoomed in on the hands, and began to film.

Meanwhile Hamilton made his way back to where he had left Sheppard and Taylor, only slightly more slowly than before. "Malcolm!" he shouted while still a dozen yards away. "Get Maureen Slattery here."

Sheppard looked confused. "The telephonist?"

"Yes. And make it fast. Motorcycle escort - use the helicopter if you have to - but get her here ten minutes ago."

"Yes sir." Sheppard only ever called his Chief Constable "Sir" when he disagreed with him or, as now, had no idea what he was talking about and suspected that his well known eccentricity was taking supremacy over his reason. Hamilton could call in experts on everything from explosives to scuba-diving; but he wanted a switchboard operator. Still, Sheppard knew better than to question the order, and if Hamilton wanted Maureen Slattery he would have her. The Chief, he decided, as he hurried into the command vehicle and grabbed the phone, must know something he didn't. Perhaps she was was into telepathy as well as telephony.

The orders given, he returned to Hamilton and was secretly pleased to see that Commander Taylor was obviously as baffled as he was, but was too proud to ask and tried to mask this by staring intently through the binoculars.

The Chief Constable stood stock still, his binoculars also clamped to his eyes. "Know your staff, Malcolm," he said, without moving.

"Every one of them. Mrs. Slattery's husband is deaf. Did you know that?"

Malcolm and Taylor now both looked at him as though fearing for his sanity.

"The hands, man. The hands."

Malcolm looked back towards the window across the street. "He's fidgeting. Yes."

"Not fidgeting - he's signalling. Talking to us. Somewhere along the line, Robert, your Mr. Lamb has learned to finger spell. I know a bit of it myself, but only the odd letter. And doing it behind his back

7

with his hands tied makes it difficult to read. But if that TV man does his job, an expert like Mrs. Slattery should be able to tell us exactly what he's saying."

"Well I'll be damned." Taylor put the glasses back to his eyes and looked again. "Good for you, Neil," he said, softly. "Good for you."

"You have to admire him," Malcolm agreed. "In a spot like that. Even to think of it is brilliant. Should we let him know we've seen it?"

Taylor shook his head. "I can't see how we can without alerting his captors."

Maureen Slattery did not arrive by helicopter, but she arrived very quickly by car with a motorcycle escort. She had no idea why she'd been summoned, since Malcolm had not known himself when he sent for her, and she was flustered and a little white as she was helped out. An unscheduled trip in a high speed pursuit vehicle is an unnerving experience for the uninitiated.

The driver escorted her over to where Malcolm and the two others stood, and her discomfiture was in no way diminished by finding herself suddenly the centre of attention in such a high-powered gathering. Hamilton greeted her warmly and attempted to put her at her ease.

The figure of Neil Lamb had vanished from the window opposite, and all that was left was the video of his hands. The cameraman had moved his equipment into the command trailer, and wired it up to a monitor ready to roll. Hamilton escorted Maureen Slattery into the vehicle, explaining as they went why he had sent for her. She sat down in front of the screen, and within four minutes of her arrival was peering at the image of two writhing hands desperately twisting and straining to contort themselves into the shapes of the letters agreed by international convention and used by deaf people the world over. She watched the whole thing through without a word, while every other eye in the place studied her face, anxious for a clue as to how much information she could distil from what she saw. When it ended, with the hands disappearing suddenly as their owner was tugged roughly out of sight, she sat back with a frown of worry and concentration on her face.

8

"Well he's finger spelling all right - or at least he's trying to - but it's not very clear, I'm afraid. The letters which are made at the tips of the fingers are okay - B, P, T, -and all the vowels - but the ones on the palm he can't do because the back of his right hand is in the way of his left.

"And he's rushing, not putting spaces between the words, so it just comes across as a jumble of unintelligible letters." She turned to the cameraman, who was re-winding the tape. "Can we see it more slowly?"

"No problem."

Malcolm picked up the pad of paper and pen that had been laid out in readiness, and said: "Call out the letters and I'll write them down."

Maureen peered at the screen, and with Hamilton and Taylor looking over his shoulders Malcolm began taking the slow dictation.

"I, C, - hang on. Can I see that again?" The cameraman stopped the tape, and rewound briefly.Maureen watched again. "No. I've no idea what that is. Carry on. Sorry - can you stop again? Two straight fingers together. You see that could be an F or an N, depending on where he put them, but he can't put them anywhere, so he's just sticking them straight out."

"That's okay," Malcolm told her. "I'll put F or N and we'll work it out later."

The film started again. "One, E, pass, G, pass, E, F or N, A, C, or is it D? - I can't tell which - E, pass..." And so it continued. A number of times Maureen could not even tell how many letters there were supposed to be. "That's an M - but then again it might be two. He sort of waggles it twice... I'm not sure what he's doing here, he might be trying to make a letter or he might be just fumbling... There was a bit of a pause there. I don't know if it means anything... Now what's he doing here? He's flapping his hand. Is that meant to be a one-handed H or is he saying he's made a mistake? Wiping out the last letter? I'm sorry - I'm not doing very well."

"You're doing fine," her Chief Constable assured her.

When the film finally flickered to a stop the message on Malcolm's page   read:

I(C/D).I(F/N)1E.G.E(F/N)A(D/C)E..I(C/D).A.(D/C).A..E(F/N)(D/C)E

.B?A..AL
LIO(F/N).O(F/N)??GAIA(PAUSE?)(2/V).E(F/N)AU.OM??A.I(C/D).
IF(F/N)LE.?.E(
F/N)A(D/C)E..I(C/D).?A.(D/C).A..E(F/N)(D/C)E.BA..ALLIO(F/N).O
(F/N)GAIA(PAUSE?)(2/V).E?(F/N)A

"There's a repeat between the pauses," Taylor said immediately. "He's repeating the same message over and over."

Malcolm put the pad down on the desk and the three of them bent over it. "That could be 'automatic'." Taylor pointed. "And what's this? 'o(f/n)gaia'." He turned to Maureen. "Are you sure about that? It doesn't sound like English."

"Yes it is," Malcolm contradicted before she could answer. "That's Gaia, as in the Battalions of Gaia, the environmentalist group."

Even as he spoke he realised what he had said, but it was Hamilton who put it into words. "That's it! It fits. 'Battalions of Gaia'." He stabbed at the sheet with his finger.

Malcolm looked puzzled. So what's he saying then? That there's a tie-up between these terrorists and the Battalions of Gaia?"

"I hope not," an inspector interrupted. "My daughter's in the Battalions of Gaia. They're not terrorists. Not unless you count waving a few banners as terrorism."

"So's my nephew," Taylor agreed. "But that doesn't mean there can't be some connection. Perhaps the PFLPE are a fringe element. Or perhaps they are trying to infiltrate them. Whatever it is it must be pretty important - that man's life is on the line; he wouldn't be telling us if he didn't think it was crucial. What else is there?"

Again they poured over the jumble of letters. "'Automatic' what? What could he be saying?"

"Guns? Weapons?"

"'Rifles' would fit."

"Right. 'Automatic rifles...' Perhaps he's telling us what to expect when we go in there to get him." Everyone in the trailer was now working on the puzzle. Each had a piece of paper and a pen and were busily computing possible combinations."

"'Grenades'," a woman sergeant shouted out from the back. It was checked and agreed.

"And if it's a 2 not a V then '2 men' would fit and make sense," Hamilton suggested.

"Got to be," Taylor agreed. "'Two men, automatic rifles, grenades ... Battalions of Gaia. So what's the bit in the middle? .I(C/D).A.(D/C).A..E(F/N)(D/C)E.?"

They worked away at it without success. The tape was replayed three more times to see if Maureen could get any other letters, but it was useless. The best guess was that it might be a name or names, but they could not even get close, and eventually they had to give up. They went outside to find the negotiators from the Met had turned up and were being briefed on the situation.

For five hours there was no progress. All attempts to engage the kidnappers in dialogue failed, and neither Neil Lamb nor anyone else appeared at any of the windows. Then, at 5.47 pm, the sound of a single shot was heard, muffled, from somewhere within the building. The air of boredom that had settled on the encampment was shattered by the sound - the watching marksmen shifted their stances and sighted their weapons, and a hubbub of conversation broke out among the others as the significance of this development was explored, and alternatives to the obvious were sought.

If Lamb was dead, there was nothing to stop them swarming the building, but they could not be sure. It could have been a warning, an accident, or even a trap. So they continued to wait, the negotiators occasionally addressing the house through loudhailers - they had long ago established that there was no reply to the phone number suppled for the address by British Telecom - in a vain attempt to draw a response.

The explosion came at 6.32. The upstairs window at which Lamb had made his brief appearance burst outwards, showering the watchers across the road with shards of broken glass and splinters of timber, sending everyone diving for cover.

When the shower ended, and silence returned, the shaken officers brushed debris from their clothing, and once again broke into urgent discussion, those with keener hearing asserting they had heard a double explosion. Hamilton bent down, and, from the ground at his feet, carefully picked up a fragment of metal in his gloved hand. He showed it to Taylor. "What do you make of that, Commander?"

"Hand grenade."

The Chief nodded his agreement, and looked across at the hole where the window had been. "Possibly two?"

"One or two, there'll be nobody left in that room." Taylor said bitterly.

"If there was anyone in there. Could it have been a ruse to lure us in, do you think?"

Taylor considered. "I don't see why. If they wanted to do that they only had to talk to the negotiators and invite them in."

"So it's time to go?"

"Yes."

It was a slow process - each move had to be checked and covered, and the possibility of booby traps explored at every step - but they made their way in through the back of the building and eventually found themselves at the head of the stairs, certain now that there was no-one left alive in the house. The front bedroom, from which the explosion had come, they entered last, and even for men hardened to the ways of the world it was not easy opening that door, knowing what the room had to contain.

The only consolation to be had afterwards was that Neil Lamb almost certainly died quickly from a single bullet. As for the men who had killed him, little would ever be known. The final, expert analysis of the remains was that they had lain on the floor, close together, head to toe. Each had clasped a hand-grenade to their head, and they had pulled the pins and released the plungers simultaneously. By this ruthless, fanatical self-sacrifice they had obliterated their faces, dental records, fingerprints and even toe prints.

Back in the mobile HQ the three top men had a brief discussion - there was not a great deal to say. The siege was over, and a police officer had been killed. Not enough remained of the killers to offer any realistic hope that the forensic work, which would continue for weeks, would identify them. All that was left, the only thing they had to go on, was Lamb's reference to an apparently innocuous group of environmentalists, and possibly a name, which they could not read.

"I'll get the image enhancers to work on the film, and we'll have the best people available look at it," Hamilton promised. "But I'm not hopeful they'll get any more than Maureen has. It's not a lot to go on."

"Too damn little," Taylor growled through a clenched jaw. He had lost men in the field before, but that did not make it one iota less damnable. "But I'll get who's behind this. That is a promise."

"Keep in touch," Hamilton told him, as he prepared to leave. "You'll be the first to know if we come up with anything on the film." The rivalry between the two men had evaporated. A police officer had been killed, and it did not matter which branch he came from. Until the identity of the men who's remains had been sprayed over Lamb's body was known there would be nothing but cooperation between Mr. Hamilton and Cdr. Taylor.

CHAPTER 1

The alarm clock mewed twice, very quietly. Left to its own devices it would have built up to a crescendo that could be heard downstairs, but, as always, its owner's hand snaked out from beneath the sheets like some alert reptile that had been lying in wait, and silenced it.

Rory Kilbride slipped out of the bed, carefully replacing the covers so as not to wake the other occupant. He looked down at the head nestling on the pillow, kissed the tip of his finger, and touched her forehead. She stirred and snuggled deeper under the duvet. He collected his clothes and went through to the bathroom to dress.

Seventy minutes later he was driving past Bien Diarg. As journeys to work go this one took a lot of beating, and he smiled as he watched the first rays of the morning sun bring the mist swirling up from the river Lyon on his left.

Half way down between Bridge of Balgie and Loch Daimn he took a turning off to the left, onto a small, though well-metalled track, marked only by a 'No Through Road' sign. He followed it up, over a saddle between two rocky outcrops and then down, out of sight of the main road. A mile later he arrived at work.

The Chemical Defence Establishment at Lairig a' Mhuic in the Grampian Region of Scotland is less well known than its sister institution at Porton Down only because it is remote, and more easily kept out of the public eye, and therefore its mind. From the perimeter fence, at whose only gate Rory was now slowing his Astra convertible, no part of the development was visible, and signs stating that the land beyond was a weapons training area patrolled by guard dogs was enough to put off the most inquisitive rambler. He wound down the window and handed Terry Davidson his ignition keys. Terry made the brief, routine inspection of the inside of the boot before handing back the keys and reminding Rory to be punctual when he relieved him at lunch time.

Rory followed the road for another half mile till it breasted the brow of a hill and began to drop towards the strange community of scientists, and the auxiliaries who serviced their needs. Because the place was so remote, the majority lived in for the week and returned home at weekends, while those from further afield would stay for

14

weeks at a time. The site, therefore, contained all the support services of a small village.

The road ran along the eastern side of the natural tarn from which the water supply was taken, and as he drove the last mile Rory could see at the far end the living accommodation; five clusters of Norwegian-designed timber chalets landscaped onto the hill side among the mature Douglas Firs. Spread out below them were the school room, the recreation block, the swimming pool, and the pump house and water filtration plant. As well as servicing the pool, this latter supplied the domestic water, and the sometimes considerable requirements of the laboratories.

The octagonal recreation block was the social hub of the community, containing the canteen, restaurant, gym, squash courts, bar, pool room and library. To its south-east, across the playing field, were the three large, squat laboratory blocks, off bounds to the non-scientific support staff and fenced in on themselves; the only entrance being via the guard post at the end of the administration building. Rory drove past the turning to the stores and machine workshop, and took the next right. He pulled into the car park and climbed out, leaving the keys in the ignition. Cars did not get stolen at Lairig a' Mhuic.

At a quarter to ten he finished checking the water chlorination plant, and went to the canteen for a mid-morning coffee. As usual at this time the place was about a third full, with small groups of scientists sitting around tables animatedly talking shop. As he bought a coffee and Danish pastry, Rory spotted M.M. sitting alone, and when he had paid the highly subsidised bill, he headed over to him. So much about Charlie Wilson was out of the ordinary, the fact that he was known by initials which did not match his name was comparatively unremarkable. Standing behind a fruit and veg stall in Bethnal Green he would have blended into the scenery, but in the rarefied atmosphere of the international scientific elite this stocky, cheerful, prematurely white haired cockney was as inconspicuous as a juke box in a cathedral. Unlike many provincial proteges who make it to the top, he had passed through Cambridge and Harvard making no attempt to trade in his accent for a more fashionable one, addressing everyone, high and low, as "me old mate". He had continued his career, collecting two honorary doctorates and a Fellowship of the Max Planck Institute on the way, without losing anything of his easy-going East End warmth. New acquaintances, from grandees to gatekeepers, were liable to come away from their introductory handshake clasping a porcelain egg; which fact accounted for the initials. M.M. stood for "Mr. Mysterio", in which persona Dr. Charlie Wilson, eminent scientist and paid up member of the Magic Circle, entertained children and adults alike at any appropriate gathering.

"Morning Rory."

"Morning M.M." Rory placed his purchases on the table. "You look thoughtful - is it something good?

"It's a stinker. 'Thee' - three, four, three, four, five."

"That all?"

"Yup."

Another of Charlie Wilson's attributes was that he had a truly photographic memory. He could look at a page of a book for a few seconds, without taking anything in, and an hour later recall it to mind and read the words. Believing this to be a gift which would wither if not regularly used, he practised it by imprinting the Times crossword each morning, and mentally completing it in leisure moments during the day.

Sometimes he and Rory, who also enjoyed a crossword, would swap particularly pleasing solutions or help each other out - though Rory would have been the first to admit that this was normally a one-sided exchange. The number of times he solved a clue which had stumped M.M. could have been counted on the legs of the table.

"Have you got any letters?" Rory asked.

"Yes. I'll write them down." He reached for a paper napkin and wrote on it: _ _ _ W_ _ _ T_ E _ E_ _ T_ _ _ S. He passed it over to Rory.

"You'd think it ought to be something like 'The old word for ....'. Presumably the third word is 'the'."

"Yes. Although it could conceivably be 'toe', tie', or even 'tee'."

Rory nodded. "I hate it when there's nothing to work on. You either get it or you don't."

"There is that song." Charlie hummed "... take off your something, your coat and your glove, and come with me for thee I love."

"Yes. I don't know any more words of it." He thought. "What about: 'I plight thee my troth'?"

"That's a possibility. 'She whom the ....'" They continued to play around with it until Charlie looked at his watch and started to rise. "Keep at it me old mate. It'll come to one of us sooner of later. Oh, by the way - you haven't seen Skinner or Dobbs have you?"

"No. Do you need them?"

"Not particularly. It's just that I went to their lab to borrow something, and they weren't there. I've asked around and nobody seems to have seen them today."

"They may have rung in. I'll check with Mr. McLennan."

"Right. Though it's not urgent from my point of view."

Rory drank his Cappuccino and completed a third of his own crossword, and when he had finished walked over to the Administration block and knocked on the door marked: "Duncan McLennan - Chief Security Officer." He popped his head round the door.

"Morning Rory. Come on in."

"Morning Duncan. Nothing major, but M.M. says that no-one has seen Dr. Skinner or Dr. Dobbs today. He wondered if they'd rung in."

"Nope." McLennan removed a book from a drawer in his desk, and consulted it. "Neither of them is booked out. You're sure they're not here?"

"I only know what Dr. Wilson said."

"Mmm. Check with the gate, would you?"

Rory took the radio from its harness on his belt and pressed a button. "Hello, Terry, it's Rory. Have Drs. Skinner or Dobbs come in today? ... I see. They did leave yesterday, did they? ... Right, okay. Thanks." He put the radio away. "No joy. They left at just gone seven last night, but they haven't come in today."

McLennan took another book from his top drawer, looked up a number, and rang it. He let it ring for several minutes, then put down the receiver. "No answer from their house," he said, furrowing his brow. "Odd. I hope they haven't had an accident on the way in."

"I don't suppose the place will grind to a halt without them," Rory said lightly. It was an open secret that the two elderly scientists were coasting downhill to retirement. Working together they had been big names in the sixties; at the cutting edge of science. They had continued to do good work in the seventies and eighties, building on their reputations as widely respected and frequently published innovators in the field of molecular engineering. But science advances at a pace which overtakes even the most capable mind eventually, and with new, young blood coming in at the bottom teeming with new ideas and versed in the latest technologies, those at the mature end of things often look to administrative posts and directorships to absorb their talents. But neither Paul Skinner nor Norman Dobbs had any inclination in this direction, nor interest in anything but their work. Since they had already paid their way as time-serving government employees, as they headed now towards retirement they had been left the freedom of the laboratory they had shared for nearly as long as it had been built, to explore whatever profitless channels took their fancy.

"I don't suppose it will," McLennan agreed. "But nevertheless, this is a defence establishment and I am responsible for the security of the personnel. I think I'll go over to their place and check it out."

Skinner and Dobbs were among the few people who, like Rory himself, chose to commute, and among the boffins they were unique in that they had bought a house a few miles out of Strathtay, and drove in daily.

Duncan McLennan took his car, and drove the twenty miles to Aberfeldy retracing the route Rory had driven earlier. On the outskirts he turned left, and followed a minor road that twisted and turned away from the town until he reached the solid, dressed stone house that stood somewhat forlornly in the wilderness of what had once been an interesting terraced garden, but which had been wholly neglected by the two ageing scientists.

Duncan rang the door bell a number of times, and when no-one answered began scouting round the outside of the house. When he reached the large French windows which let into the capacious sitting room he discovered why the occupants of the house were not at work that day. They both lay inside on the floor, and they had both been shot through the head.

...

It was a sombre group that assembled in Graham Huish's office. Apart from Huish himself there were only four other people: the three Section heads, and Duncan McLennan.

Charlie Wilson, Miles Roper and Anthony Goodyear had no idea why the meeting had been called, but they could tell from the tone of the summons that something was wrong. As soon as they were seated Huish came straight to the point.

"I have some very sad news concerning Paul Skinner and Norman Dobbs. I am afraid they are both dead."

Lairig a' Mhuic is a small and close-knit community. Of necessity the people who work there live in close proximity with one another, eating together and playing together, as well as sharing a common purpose and the discipline of science. Skinner and Dobbs, being the longest serving of the academics, had been a part of the establishment for as long as anyone at that meeting could remember. Huish's simple, bald announcement sent a shock wave through the room.

"Dead?" It was Wilson who broke the silence. "Both of them? In the car I presume." Norman Dobbs' absent-minded performance at the wheel of the ancient Rover in which he conveyed Skinner and himself to and from work was legendary.

"No, it wasn't an accident. They were killed." Huish paused. "Shot in the head."

This time shock gave way to disbelief.

"Shot?" Miles Roper repeated automatically. "Paul and Norman? Whatever for? Who would want to shoot them? Are you sure of this, Graham?"

"I'm afraid so. It was Duncan who found them." He nodded at Charlie Wilson. "After you mentioned to Rory Kilbride that they were not at work Duncan drove over to their house."

Duncan had a tight, controlled look. He counted as friends the two men whom he had found so recently with the lower part of their heads blown over the ceiling, walls and furniture.

19

"There was no doubt whatsoever."

"It must have been a madman," Goodyear said angrily, voicing what was in most minds.

"Not necessarily." Graham Huish stared at the fountain pen he was holding for no other reason than that it gave him something to do with his hands. "There could be another reason."

"Like what?" Goodyear asked quietly.

Huish looked up at his interrogator. "It could be connected with their work."

Roper looked confused. "But I thought you effectively pensioned them off after the PRND project was completed."

"I did. With Norman's poor health and the fact that they both had less than a year to go to retirement, I left them to their own devices."

"So what have they been up to?"

"That's the problem. It seems they decided to go back over their work on Teronin, in the light of modern techniques."

"Ah. I see." So did the other two scientists present. Back in the sixties Skinner and Dobbs headed the team which had come up with Teronin, one of the series of nerve agents - Tabun and Sarin were others - which could kill in minute quantities. "Did you know about this?"

"No. I should not have approved."

"But I still don't understand." It was Anthony Goodyear, the physicist. "That stuff's old hat now, and anyway there's gallons of it sloshing around the place waiting for someone to get round to disposing of it - not to mention what's being brewed up in their bathtubs by cranks and terrorists. What's the problem if Paul and Norman want to go back over their old notes?"

"They didn't just go back over their notes, though. They did rather more than that. Last week they told me that they had restructured the agent, using the latest molecular engineering techniques, into long-chain cluster molecules. They believed that just one of these molecules could be fatal."

A stunned silence fell on the room, which Charlie Wilson tried to break with a profanity, but though he mouthed the words no sound came out. Only Duncan looked less than dumbfounded.

"I think I'm missing something here; could someone enlighten me? I'm sure it is very clever scientifically speaking, but a tiny droplet of Teronin, inhaled or in contact with the skin, is fatal. I don't see why there is such a big difference between being killed by lots of small molecules, or one big one."

Sir Graham Huish nodded understandingly. "We scientists regularly deal in concepts and numbers which we take for granted, but which have no meaning for other people. You are right, of course, a small droplet of any of the major nerve agents can be sufficient to kill. But such a droplet contains molecules in numbers you cannot conceive of.

"Let me give you an example. Paul and Norman made just under half a pint of their new concoction - let's call it Teronin 2. Suppose I put that in a coffee mug, and took it down to the Firth of Lorn and poured it into the sea. If you stirred up all the oceans of the world thoroughly you could go anywhere on the planet, scoop out a bucketful of water, and it would contain at least one molecule of T2. And that molecule would kill you.

"Or to put it another way: even though these are large and comparatively heavy molecules, a millionth of an ounce would be enough to give something like a thousand million lethal doses to every man, woman and child on the earth."

Duncan's already drawn face lost even more of its colour. "Thank you," he said very quietly. "Now I understand."

Huish looked at him and shook his head. "Unfortunately", he said, very slowly, "I'm not sure that you do."

Duncan raised an eyebrow. "What do you mean?"

"It's not just a matter of volume. From a military point of view all that means is that you need less of it - a few cc instead of tons. But we have adequate delivery systems, and as you said, in an area where such an agent has been deployed the air will contain so many trillions of molecules that it will hardly matter whether it takes one or ten billion to kill you.

"No, the qualitative difference is in dispersal. As you know, in a matter of hours - a day or two at most - the droplets of a conventional agent disperse. They evaporate or are diluted or simply break down

21

into quantities too small to be harmful. But this wouldn't. Each single molecule would remain a killer for the length of its life."

"Which would be how long, Graham?" Charlie had found his voice again.

"I've no idea; the stuff's only been in existence for a day or two. But anything up to a year would be a fair guess, depending on how it stands up to ultra-violet light."

"A year! Long enough for it to blow round the world a couple of times."

"At least."

"So a cloud of this would make Chernobyl look like a spring breeze?"

"There would be no comparison," Huish agreed sombrely. "The cloud from Chernobyl raised background radiation here and there, made a few sheep unfit for human consumption, and will eventually be responsible for a few thousand cancers around the world. A release of this reconstituted Teronin would kill everything in its path - well every mammal at least, I don't know what effect it would have on lower forms of life."

"And we have the only sample," Duncan said. Then added thoughtfully: "And someone knows about it."

"It certainly looks that way," Huish agreed. "It is too much of a coincidence that Norman and Paul should be murdered so soon after producing it, though who found out, and how, is unimaginable. I can't believe they would have told anyone, and as far as I am aware I was the only other person who knew about it."

"Well it looks as though someone has not only found out, but what's more wants to get their hands on it," Duncan said.

Charlie Wilson looked baffled. "But why shoot Paul or Norman? Surely they'd want to keep them alive?"

"There could be several reasons," Duncan suggested. "Perhaps they were trying to force or bribe them to smuggle the stuff out and they refused. They might have feared they would go to the authorities. It's possibly Paul and Norman knew them, or perhaps they simply wanted to know where the sample was so they could steal it. If they had found that out they could do without Paul and Norman." He turned to Huish. "What about the formula? Could they have extracted the knowledge of how to make the stuff themselves?"

"Highly unlikely. A process like that is immensely complex - it would require a small book to explain it, and I have their notes locked up in my safe."

Miles Roper was sitting tapping the top of a pencil on the desk. "Look," he said carefully, "we could be getting ahead of ourselves here. Paul and Norman were first class scientists, and we are all shocked by their deaths, but we shouldn't get carried away. If what you claim for this is true it is a fantastic scientific achievement, but I have to say I find it almost too much to believe. If they were alive we wouldn't even begin to get excited about it until the procedure had been independently replicated by another team. Paul and Norman would have been the first to want that, and we owe it to them to check it out properly." He turned to Huish. "Give me six months, Graham. I'll put a team together and start work right away."

"No." Huish was so emphatic that Roper, who was, after all only proposing the normal scientific procedure, was taken aback. "This is too dangerous. I might agree if security had not already been breached, but given that someone knows about it and appears to be after it, I want it destroyed."

"Destroyed! But Graham, that's sacrilege. If they *are* right this is a major piece of work."

"I'm sorry, Miles. Scientifically it may be pure genius, but from a military point of view it is useless. It could never be deployed, and I believe it's too dangerous to hang on to, even for the sake of scientific research, "

Roper opened his mouth to remonstrate, but closed it again. In the silence that followed Duncan turned to Huish and said, "Where is the sample now?"

"In my safe."

"About half a pint?"

"Yes."

"And that's all there is? Can we destroy it here?"

"Yes to the former, no to the latter. We don't know how to do that. It will have to go to an incinerator. Johnston Island, I would think, given the degree of risk."

Duncan nodded, he knew of it. The tiny volcanic speck in the middle of the Pacific where the US had its largely experimental high temperature facility for destroying the West's unwanted stockpile of ageing, unstable chemical weapons. It was well-placed from the Americans' point of view, since the products of any incomplete combustion or accidental discharges would blow over a few neighbouring islands, well away from the US itself. This arrangement had never seemed to have such an appeal for the governments and people of the islands concerned.

"Will they accept it?"

"They'll have to. What alternatives are there? No-one is going to be safe until it's been disposed of."

"How do you intend to get it there?"

"There is a consignment of Sarin due for shipment to Johnston in a couple of weeks. It is going on the frigate *Lysander*. I shall simply say that we have a particularly unstable, experimental sample, that we want included and which needs special care."

"And what will you tell the Americans?"

"The same. Johnston is the best place they have - the best anyone has. Since they can't do better than their best, telling them they are dealing with liquid Armageddon isn't going to make it any safer. And it is in everyone's interest for as few people to know as possible. So I want to keep this strictly in-house." He looked round at the others. "I have told the four of you because I have to. Paul and Norman's deaths are naturally going to raise a great deal of concern here, and a lot of questions will be asked. I want you to help in fielding these as far as possible.

"And there's another thing - secondary but still important. This whole episode would be highly embarrassing if it leaked out - for me, for this establishment, and the Government. We are supposed to be observing a moratorium on R & D into chemical weapons. Our detractors would have a field day, and the Government would be forced to be seen to do something about it. I do not want that to happen." He looked again, slowly, at each of his colleagues. "I hardly need to point out that there has never been a time when it was more important to be absolutely scrupulous about what you say."

24

A solemn nodding of heads implied that the seriousness of the situation was impressed on all concerned.

"One more question," Duncan said. "In the event of a worst case scenario, is there any antidote to this substance?"

"The only known general prophylactic for nerve agent contamination is pyridostigmine bromide taken every eight hours, or post-exposure injections of atropine sulphate and pralidoxime mesylate taken in conjunction with diazepam. Whether they would have any effect on this new strain is anybody's guess, and they are of very limited value at the best of times - handed out to boost morale as much as anything. I can let you have supplies of them, of course, and the crew of the *Lysander* will have their own, but as far as the public at large are concerned it's a non-starter. We can't even immunise the world's children against common childhood illnesses; we could do nothing about this on any meaningful scale."

Duncan looked at his watch. "Give me till nine tomorrow morning, and meet again here. I will have a plan of action."

At the thought of a sixty-five mile journey to and from work each day most people would reach for the Valium, but Rory Kilbride thrived on it. Faithful to the workplace lore that those from furthest away are the most punctual, he usually aimed to arrive at least forty-five minutes early, and used the time to have a meal, limber up in the gym, or socialise before going on duty.

He loved his work, and considered it a personal favour that the MoD had created the ideal job more or less on his doorstep. The full compliment of security staff at Lairig was thirty-five. There was Duncan McLennan, his deputy Ben Knight, a secretary, the two seniors - Rory himself, and Terry Davidson - and five teams each of six basic grade officers. Their brief went beyond merely guarding the place against unwanted visitors. They doubled as maintenance and ground crew, responsible for mowing and gardening, waste removal, fire safety and the maintenance and supervision of the swimming pool. They also offered fitness instruction to the scientists and their families, and when required ran sports sessions and cycling proficiency classes for any children in residence. This arrangement had a two-fold advantage: it halved the bureaucracy and allowed greater flexibility, giving McLennan a larger force than would otherwise be possible on which he could call for security purposes if the need arose. It also made for variety, thus keeping his staff fresh and alert.

As for the long drive home, for Rory that was just one more perk. Not for him the semi-permanent traffic jams that inch their way infuriatingly through congested streets of tense, irritable drivers fidgeting helplessly in their steel cages. He swept unhindered through some of the most austerely beautiful scenery in the world. Born and bred in the Grampians he had that fey, almost symbiotic relationship with the landscape which is characteristic of the highland Scot, and driving through it at the end of the working day had a calming, restorative effect. His staggered shift patterns meant he sometimes made the journey at two in the morning, sometimes two in the afternoon, or anywhere in between, driving in all but the most inclement weather with the top of his car down, revelling in the caress of the mountain air.

From season to season the majestic oil painting of a landscape through which he passed changed subtly in tone and hue. He watched the heathers bloom and fade, the bracken turn to green to brown to green again, the bilberries ripen and drop, and the snows fall and melt. But underneath this shifting kaleidoscope of colour nothing altered. The rough-hewn granite contours stood unchanged and unchangeable, each crag and brae, each scaur and escarpment, exactly as it was when his grandfather had first taught him their names, and as they would be when he taught his grandchildren, and they theirs, till the end of time.

Perhaps it was the landscape that made it so hard to believe Hannah's prophesies of doom. He didn't doubt the facts and figures she brought home from her meetings, about ozone holes and acid rain and greenhouse gas and the like. He knew he lived in a rapidly changing, unstable world; after all, the work of Lairig a' Mhuic - of which he was a small part - reflected the distrust and instability that characterised world affairs, and added all the time to man's ability to destroy his fellow man. Yet driving through this familiar, solid landscape he felt himself a part of the life which clung to the bedrock of the planet, ebbing and flowing through the storms of winter and the heat of summer; but always surviving.

It was half past six as he reached Crieff. Hannah would be back from the university by now; probably making her supper. The memory of her head snuggled into his pillow as he left for work brought a smile to the corners of his mouth, and he decided to visit her before going home. He drove on through Perth, and pulled to a halt outside her digs in Lochee.

She answered the door wearing jeans and a T-shirt, her feet bare, the biro behind her ear suggesting she was at work. The hair that had been tousled across his pillow in sleepy disarray was drawn back in a simple pony tail leaving her fresh, clear face unobstructed and lit from behind by the smile of greeting which sprung into being when she saw who her caller was.

"Hi. You didn't say you were coming tonight."

"I can't keep away," he smiled, entering the flat. "What time did you get up?"

"About quarter past seven."

"Half way through the day!"

"Hunh," she pouted. "By the way, your mother rang."

Rory raised an eyebrow. "Was she scandalised to find you there at that time?"

"I don't know. I told her you had let me use the flat, and that you were at work, which was true enough." She affected an air of exaggerated innocence. "I suppose I might have given her the impression you had been at work all night."

He grinned. "No point in upsetting her unnecessarily."

"Oh, and I finished your cornflakes."

"I'll buy some more. What sort of day did you have?"

"Not bad, except that we've been set another five thousand word essay for psychology. They must think we don't sleep, the amount of work they set."

"As a hard-working tax payer who funds that holiday camp you call a university, I am delighted to hear they ask some small commitment from you."

She stuck her tongue out. "It means I'll see less of you."

27

"Ah. I hadn't thought of that. Then I think it's appalling, and I shall write to your tutor and threaten to expose his regime of slavery if it doesn't stop immediately." He slumped down on the sofa and contemplated a new painting that had appeared on the wall over the elderly gas fire. It was a range of soft, rounded hills, depicted in oils by what looked like the hand of a competent amateur.

"What's the picture?"

"They're my blue remembered hills," she called from the kitchenette, where she was putting on the kettle. "My father did it."

Rory blinked, and looked again at the lush greens of the painting. "Blue remembered hills?"

She came back into the room carrying two mugs of coffee. "Did you see the film *Walkabout?*"

"I can't say I did.

She handed him his coffee and joined him on the sofa. "It was about a schoolgirl and her young brother who get lost in the Australian outback. They're just about to die when an Aborigine boy comes along and saves them. He finds food and water and leads them back to civilisation. On the way she starts to shed her western ways, but when she's faced with the choice, she returns to her own world.

"It ends with the girl grown up and married and living in this boring high-rise with a boring husband who's telling her all about his boring office job while she cooks his supper, and she goes back in her mind to when she was happy and free, swimming naked in a billabong, while a voice says:

Into my heart an air that kills, from yon far country blows.
What are those blue remembered hills?
What spires, what farms are those?
That is the land of lost content, I see it shining plain,
The happy highways where I went and cannot come again.

"I saw the film five times, and learnt the poem by heart, but I couldn't find where it came from. Whenever I saw a poetry book I used to look it up in the index, but I never found it. Then after two years I discovered what it is. And guess what?"

It was a rhetorical question which Rory made no attempt to answer. "It's about the Shropshire Hills, where I grew up. The blue remembered hills are my hills. All through my childhood they were the first thing I saw every morning when I opened my curtains, and the last thing I saw at night. When I was little I even used to talk to them."

Like many of his countrymen when it came to anything to do with hills or mountains Rory Kilbride had a romantic streak the size of Bien Leabhain. But now he turned away from the painting and shook his head slowly at its owner.

"You know I worry about you sometimes, Hannah Gentle. You are twenty, for heaven's sake, yet you talk like some octogenarian lamenting her lost youth."

"But it's not me. Don't you see - it's a metaphor. The girl represents the so-called *civilised* world, lost without her fridges and supermarkets and electricity and everything, whereas he lived in harmony with the land, living off it without destroying it. He had the power to save her, but she wouldn't be saved. Instead she destroys him. He kills himself in the end."

"Strange," he said lightly, trying to change the mood, "how all our conversations eventually come round to bottle banks and organic farming."

But he failed to puncture her intensity. "It's not that strange when you think about it. If you had been told you were going to die in the next ten minutes what do you think your main topic of conversation would be? The planet we live on is in exactly that situation.

"Talking of which I've got a Bog meeting tonight. Why don't you join me? It's your planet too, you know."

"As you never stop reminding me. What's on the agenda?"

"We have a chap coming from head office to give us an overview of the current situation. It would be a good one to come to."

He appeared to weigh it up. "It sounds interesting, but it's been a long day, and I haven't eaten yet. I think I'll give it a miss this time."

"For the umpteenth time." She looked at him despairingly. "I wonder if I'll ever get you to one."

"I expect so," he grinned. "If you try hard enough."

She made a face. "And what exactly would I have to do?"

"Oh I don't know. I expect you'll think of something."

He thought about it himself. The truth was he had nothing against looking after the environment, and while it might not have occurred to him otherwise he would have quite liked to join Hannah's Battalions of Gaia group, if only because it might have brought him closer to her. But he was not a free agent. He was in a sensitive occupation, and it would not go down well if it came to light that he was a member of a pressure group which was, by its very nature, critical of, if not opposed to, the Establishment. And it wasn't above a bit of gentle direct action and civil disobedience.

He'd never put this consideration to Hannah. For one thing it made him look a bit spineless, and for another it emphasised the differences between them, while he would prefer to concentrate on the points of contact. He was becoming quite serious about this intense, attractive young woman, and even beginning to believe they might have a future together.

"Are you coming to my place afterwards?"

"No. I've got a nine o'clock lecture in the morning. But I'll probably be there when you get home from work, though I'll have to put in some time on that essay."

He smiled, and they began the farewell they had missed out on in the morning. Twenty minutes later they went their separate ways - he home to supper, she to the Battalions of Gaia.

CHAPTER 2.

At six thirty in the morning the traffic on the M1 had already started to pick up, but business in the Watford Gap service station was slack. A handful of bleary-eyed commuters were refreshing themselves, one family was breakfasting on the way home from an out-of-season holiday, and three business reps were holding an impromptu conference in the corner.

It was their uniform that identified them as reps: smart, cautiously stylish suits over Van Heusen shirts, regulation hair just to the collar, fresh scrubbed faces shaved and perfumed, only their ties - and in one case a demur moustache and an old-fashioned watch chain - quietly understating their individuality. The younger two were probably in their mid thirties, the older one perhaps twenty years their senior. He had straight black hair and a golden ochre skin which gave him a faintly oriental look. Their business cards declared them to be Gordon Carpenter, Richard Warrender and William Yamamoto, respectively the Northern, Midlands and South East area managers of Howsafe Household Protection Ltd.

Their firm, which had been registered at Companies House four and a half years previously, specialised in supplying and fitting security equipment, intruder alarms, smoke detectors and fire extinguishers. Outside in the car park the cars they had arrived in carried the wares of their trade, and if asked to do so each could have made a decent job of a household survey, recommending and supervising the installation of a suitable system.

But then the more dedicated a terrorist the more care they go to, and these men were very dedicated indeed; zealots more in the religious mould than the political one; born again apostles of a Higher Calling. Their mission was not to redress some minor political wrong, or wrest a few acres of land from a usurping government. Their calling was nothing less than the salvation of planet Earth herself, and to that end they burned with the unshakable and total self-confidence and conviction of the rightness of their calling that is usually found only in the profoundly religious or the psychopathic.

They had come together at London University, which, like so many academic institutions at that time was a melting pot of learning, discussion and dissent, where -isms were the common currency and Protest the common language, and complacent, middle class attitudes were as comfortable as a cat in a washing machine. Toshiko William Yamamoto, lecturer in Zoology, had come over from Fukuoka University in Western Japan on a years exchange. Born in Miyakonojo in 1943 Toshiko, and his English mother, would have been liable for internment or deportation had it not been for the influence of his Japanese father. Chumi Yamamoto was a rich and powerful industrialist, and as his company was essential to the war effort, his status, and that of his family, was assured. He was a kindly man, and a good husband and father, and his relationship with his young bride was warm and close.

On the 8th August 1945 Mary Yamamoto travelled to her sister Alice's wedding; a grand affair - her fiancé was a minor nobleman - and a union blessed by both the Shinto and Roman Catholic faiths. The second ceremony took place in Japan's largest Catholic Cathedral, in Nagasaki. Mary stayed overnight, and the next day she and fifty thousand other people ceased to exist. They did not die in the normal sense; they vanished: evaporated in a fireball of ten thousand million degrees celsius, a thousand times the temperature of the sun. The 'Nuclear Age' had begun.

From then on Toshiko was raised by servants and nannies, while his widowed father buried himself in his work. When the time came, Toshiko was sent to England to study at London University and discover his English roots. He liked England where he felt a sense of nearness to the mother he could not remember, and thanks to his dual-nationality passport stayed on for ten years.

He only returned to Japan when his father suffered a stroke. Chumi was growing elderly and increasingly infirm, and Toshiko lived with him till the end, sharing the common, unspoken, regret that they had no-where to pay their respects to a woman they had both loved. They could not even visit the place where she had died, since that place itself no longer existed in any meaningful sense.

After Chumi's death Toshiko's thoughts once again began to turn to England, and, when he read of a lecturer at his old University who wanted to arrange a year's exchange, he jumped at the chance. And history repeated itself in that instead of returning to Japan after the year was up he took a permanent job and stayed on.

His study of fauna had led him to some disturbing conclusions about the future of life on the planet, and he regularly communicated these misgivings to his students, one of whom, a bright, if troubled, youth by the name of Richard Warrender, proved particularly receptive.

Richard had spent most of his childhood in Care, after his mother died in childbirth when he was four. His father, a weak man, could not cope, and handed responsibility for Richard over to the Local Authority. Doubly bereaved, by his mother's death and his father's rejection, confused, scared and bitter it was little surprise that there were problems with his placement in a foster family. After eighteen months of valiant effort they finally threw in the towel, no longer able to cope with his tantrums and destructive behaviour, and he was moved.

This further rejection only made things worse, and he entered a self-perpetuating downward spiral of deteriorating behaviour and unsuccessful placements, interspersed with frequent visits to police stations and short periods in various categories of children's homes.

He was, however, an able and intelligent child, and somehow, despite the confusion and inconsistency of his childhood, he managed to acquire sufficient qualifications to gain a place at the University.

He found there a passion for the rest of the animal kingdom which he would never feel for his fellow man, towards whom he retained a sense of bitterness which led one social worker to comment that he had enough chips on his shoulder to supply MacDonalds.

One human to whom he could relate, perhaps because they were similar personalities, perhaps because he was the strong, determined man Richard longed his father to be, was Toshihiko Yamamoto. They began attending lectures and seminars together on environmental issues. It was an area that appealed enormously to Richard: all environmental issues could be blamed on mankind, and he liked blaming things on mankind.

It was at a lecture on acid rain that the two of them met Gordon Carpenter, a second year psychology student, who shared their distrust in the ability of orthodox politics to resolve the pressing issues of a sick planet. The three men began to meet regularly.

Rapidly becoming impatient with what they saw as the complacency of existing environmental pressure groups they set to work themselves quantifying the problems and looking for solutions.

The evidence was abundant, readily accessible, and unequivocal. If the Earth was a hospital patient, they concluded it would be in Intensive Care, suffering from the cumulative effects of pollution, global warming, de-forestation, acid rain, nutrient leakage, soil erosion, rising sea levels, species depletion, dumping of toxic waste, and massive and increasing over-population.

The more they studied the phenomena the more their sense of urgency grew, for these were not discrete problems that could be resolved piecemeal, but inextricably interlinked elements in a complex, accelerating process which only a global, rigidly imposed strategy could possibly hope to bring under control.

But such a policy would be hugely unpopular politically, and anyway there were no structures by which it could be enforced.

In the end their deliberations led to one inescapable conclusion: the crux of the problem was population growth. People require food, shelter, warmth, education, employment and transport, and with the numbers inexorably growing, so the planet had to be pillaged more and more to meet these requirements. Yet even the most optimistic forecasts envisaged world population continuing to grow for at least another century. Everything the three men learned from their detailed analyses suggested that in a matter of only a few decades large parts of the world would either have disappeared beneath the rising oceans or been rendered virtually uninhabitable, able to sustain only the sparsest of populations living a very basic existence. The inhabitants of these areas would become refugees, forced to migrate in search of new homes. When the numbers became critical wars would ensue, but countries involved in warfare have even less time and money and resources to devote to environmental problems.

And the process was so clearly under way it was unbelievable the world at large seemed either ignorant or indifferent to it. It was Gordon Carpenter, the psychology student, who pointed out that this denial was not only consistent with human nature but virtually inevitable. When a problem is inescapable people either block it out or risk losing their minds. If people can live equanimously on the San Andreas fault or at the foot of an active volcano, why should it be surprising that others can turn a blind eye to acid rain or global warming?

As they pursued this analysis they began to question at a fundamental level their evaluation of themselves and the world in which they lived. The accepted view of the human race as the pinnacle of evolution gave way to an image of a profligate and unruly child whose selfish and irresponsible behaviour was ravaging the beautiful and abundant biosphere of which it saw itself as the only important inhabitant. Influenced by the work of James Lovelock, and his theory of Gaia - the Earth herself as a living, breathing being, with rivers for arteries, water for blood, and forests for lungs - they came to view the human race as her most destructive parasite.

It might be ignorance rather than malice that had created the situation, but unless and until it was universally acknowledged that the environmental imperative must take priority over all else the problem would not be redressed. Mankind had to come to see itself and its needs and desires, however legitimate, as subservient to those of the Earth.

And it was thus they moved into territory more normally occupied by religion. Gaia was the Earth Mother. She gave life. Mankind had come from the dust of the Earth, and to it would return, and in the brief meantime She supplied every meal, every drop of water, every molecule of air breathed. Down the ages people have willingly laid down their lives to please their gods: what would one not do for a god who was dying?

Or rather being killed. Murdered by her own delinquent children; choked, strangled and poisoned by the very ones she had spawned and nurtured?

Having identified the scale of the problem their late night brainstorming sessions turned to the response. They had no illusions about stopping the world in its self-destructive tracks, but matters would bring themselves to a head quite soon enough without any help from them. And at times of crisis people who are normally conservative and obdurate become open to change. The three would develop a crisis intervention plan which would enable them to steer events once they became sufficiently fluid.

The first priority was a power base, and it was thus that the Battalions of Gaia was born. With the immediate threat of a nuclear holocaust dramatically reduced in the public mind by the break up of the Soviet Union, the nation was hungry for a cause onto which to transfer its collective angst, and the gang of three deliberately – (detractors would say cynically) - set about creating a designer pressure group to exploit and channel this mood. Realising that their more extreme, apocalyptic beliefs would alienate those who had not had the chance to sift the evidence and reach their own conclusions, they set out their stall modestly, establishing a broad church with no catechism or credo, but a generous pick-'n-mix menu from which anyone with a concern for the environment could select something to their taste.

It was not hard to get the movement going; in the hothouse atmosphere they lived and studied is it was not long before they found themselves at the centre of an ever-growing caucus which in turn rapidly spread beyond the University. They welcomed all-comers, while carefully sifting the serious proselytes from the fashion-seekers, and grooming them for future leadership.

The organisation's logo, a picture of the world as seen from space in its swirling greens and blues and white, surrounded by the outline of a dustbin, was exploited to create product identification, with badges, T shirts and tie pins, and the acronym BoG was used to good advantage; their followers gleefully adopting the term 'boggers' before their detractors could beat them to it.

The movement was based on small, local groups, and the social side of things promoted as strongly, if not more so, than the business side. Their objective was to draw in as many people as possible, create a sense of identity and belonging, and at the same time educate them towards the truths which they had themselves reached. But this was only the beginning.

As they put their plan into operation, and cells began springing up around the country, the three faded gradually out of sight, leaving their most promising disciples to run the organisation and put their names on the letterheads and applications for charitable status. Those who noticed their departure assumed a difference of opinion, a boardroom coup, or simply loss of interest. The ever-growing membership was unaware that the three retained control, but exercised it now unseen, from behind the throne.

Thus removed from the glare of public scrutiny, and financed from the membership fees and fund-raising activities of the organisation, the three were free to pursue their own, more direct crusade against the forces of destruction. The end to which they worked - the salvation of the planet and, *inter alia,* of mankind itself - justified any means, and they shrank from no opportunity to raise public awareness of the immediacy of the impending nightmare. They had carried out five bombings - two at major chemical plants, one at the holiday home of the Energy Secretary, one which blew up a lorry-load of imported hardwood, and one which made a large crater in a new motorway. On each occasion the reason for their protest was phoned to Scotland Yard and accredited to the Popular Front for the Liberation of Planet Earth. They took great care to ensure that the PFLPE should not be connected with the Battalions of Gaia, which was tolerated by the Establishment as probably doing nothing worse than channelling the enthusiasm and energy of youth into a relatively harmless cul-de-sac.

But this campaign of sporadic, violent protest was designed only to keep environmental matters in the public eye, and to keep the powers that be on their toes. They knew that it alone could not win their cause; nor did it have to.

Every belief system has some future event to anticipate, whether it is the visitation of its prophet, the second coming, the revolution to end all revolutions, or the end of the world. For the gang of three, and their disciples, it was the collapse of the earth's biosphere, and it was imminent and obvious. It was not dependent on a belief in ancient writings or prophesies, nor the haruspications of some German economist; it was clear and visible and openly reported and discussed. The greenhouse effect was overheating the atmosphere; the great forests - the only natural resource large enough to counter this - were being burnt and flattened, and killed with acid rain at a staggering rate; the seas were dying from pollution and toxic waste, and growing over with rafts of oxygen-excluding algae fed by the runoff of overused agricultural fertilisers.

And the response of governments to this made Nero's musical activity during the conflagration of Rome seem positively masterful. How long did people think this self-fuelling spiral of destruction could continue before it went critical - before the planet died? Most likely they would come to their senses at the eleventh hour and start casting around for some miracle to save them.

And the Battalions of Gaia would be ready; they would be that miracle. They would have the infrastructure, the people - the membership would grow and become increasingly radical as events unfolded - and they would have blueprints for the alternative economies and technologies which alone could save the planet and at least some of its inhabitants. The world would turn to them because it would have nowhere else to go.

Richard Warrender took a sip of his orange juice, glanced around the cafeteria to check that no-one was within earshot, and then addressed the man sitting opposite him.

"Okay Gordon, what have you come to share with us?"

Gordon Carpenter double checked that they were not overheard, looked at each of his colleagues in turn, as though not sure where to start, and then began slowly in a voice so low as to be barely audible: "I had a visit from my contact at Lairig a' Mhuic. There's something very big going on there."

"What sort of thing?"

"It seems they have produced a super strain of nerve gas, more powerful than anything previously. It is ... well I gather Sir Graham Huish, the Director of Lairig a' Mhuic, described it as "Armageddon in a jam jar", and he's worked with chemical weapons most of his life. He's not a man given to overstatement."

Toshiko Yamamoto creased his brow. "What are they doing making new chemical weapons? There's a moratorium on all development and manufacture."

"Exactly. That's why this is political dynamite. If we could expose it we would catch the government with its trousers round its ankles. The international repercussions would be immense. World-wide coverage."

"I like it." Warrender took another sip of juice. "Can you get proof? They'll deny it till they're blue in the face otherwise."

"I doubt it, though I suppose if the stakes were high enough I might get my contact to go public. But there's another thing."

"What's that?"

"Someone else knows. They've killed the two scientists who invented it. The deaths have been hushed up, but it looks as though whoever killed them is planning to steal the stuff."

"Any ideas who it is?"

"None at all."

There was a pause while they digested the information, and considered the ramifications. Eventually Yamamoto said: "Suppose we could beat them to it...?"

"You must be joking, Tosh. They're protecting it better than the crown jewels. And anyway, there's only half a pint in existence, and they're sending that away to be destroyed."

"But you say someone else is planning to liberate it - so why not us?

There was another silence. Eventually Toshiko muttered quietly: "Whoever had it could demand just about anything! Stop all deforestation immediately, or ban greenhouse gas emissions, or artificial fertilisers, or private cars, or road building, or close all nuclear power stations...." He shook his head, realising what he was saying.

"Don't be crazy." Carpenter had not had this in mind when he summoned the others to the meeting. "They could never afford to agree."

"What alternative would they have?"

"They'd think of something. For starters they'd put every law enforcement agency in the world onto it: CIA, FBI, MI5, Interpol, KGB and Old Uncle Tom Cobbley and all, giving the job their undivided attention?"

"And what would they do? If all we had to do was take off with a jam jar? How would they find us?"

"Hang on." It was Richard Warrender, the unelected leader of the group, who brought them back to reality. "Let's put the horse back in

39

front of the cart for just a moment, shall we, and take this one step at a time? First of all, how good is your contact, Gordon?"

"Absolutely sound. He's a believer; one of us."

"All right. So exactly what has he told you?"

"The stuff was made unofficially. They're embarrassed about it, and planning to send it to the incinerator on Johnston Atoll to be destroyed."

"How?"

"He doesn't know, but he will soon. And they're going to do it as quickly as possible. It's not just an embarrassment, they're all scared stiff of it."

"Wouldn't you be?" Warrender thought for a moment. "They won't fly it; too risky. So, road or rail, and then boat."

Toshiko Yamamoto looked across at him, his eyes questioning. Hopeful. "Do you think there's a chance of taking it?"

Warrender shrugged. "There is always a chance - if we decided to go for it."

"But we have to, don't we? It's the opportunity of a lifetime."

Warrender puckered his lips thoughtfully. "We have a man on the inside." He looked at Carpenter again. "Do we have any other levers, Gordon?"

"Possibly, yes. There's a member of our Dundee branch who's having it off with one of the security guards. We might be able to apply a bit of pressure there."

"We might indeed. The omens do seem to be encouraging." Warrender looked at his colleagues. It was clear what Tosh thought; he faced Gordon.

"We go for it?" he asked.

Gordon Carpenter looked doubtful. "I don't know. The odds are absurdly long." He shrugged. "I suppose there'd be nothing to lose by making a preliminary recce."

"Right," Warrender said decisively. "Tosh, can you put together an outline plan of action for liberating the stuff?"

"Will do."

"You will need to consult with Gordon over his contacts, and you'll need help. But don't involve any more people than you need to. I will look at what we would do if we got it: where to hide it - and ourselves - and laboratory facilities to dilute it and and break it down into small units.

"Gordon, can you do something on how we could best use it? What demands to make? Timetables etc?"

"No problem."

"Good. We'll meet again at the office tomorrow evening."

...

Everyone was in place in Huish's office promptly at nine o'clock, and Duncan McLennan, his eyes rimmed from a sleepless night, went straight to business.

"Firstly, Sir Graham has been on to the Minister. He wants total secrecy on this - no-one is to be told of the existence of the new form of Teronin who does not already know." He looked briefly round. "I will not insult you by reminding you that that request is legally binding and that you have each signed the Official Secrets Act.

"I then phoned the Chief Constable, and without going into details persuaded him to sit on the press over the deaths of Drs. Skinner and Dobbs. He can't cover them up, but he will put it out that there are no suspicious circumstances and it is believed to be a suicide pact. The police will also be helping with transport, but I'll come to that.

"I then spoke to the MoD. As Graham said there is a consignment of chemical weapons being shipped to Johnston Atoll a week tomorrow. It sails from Aberdeen on the frigate *Lysander*. I intend to add the T2 to that shipment. The captain will be told that it is a particularly virulent and unstable agent, but no more than that.

"We then have the question of how to get the T2 to Aberdeen. We could call in the army, but on balance I am against that, and so is the Minister. A big operation would simply advertise its whereabouts, and we can never guarantee a hundred per cent security against a terrorist who wants publicity. We can't close off every road between here and Aberdeen, remove every parked vehicle that might be booby-trapped along the way, or defend against mortar or rocket attack. So this is what I propose:"

He picked up a stainless steel cylinder, eight inches in diameter by fourteen high, which had been sitting on Huish's desk. "You will all recognise this as a standard TCR." The Toxic Commodity Receptacle was a tool of their trade. The airtight lid of the cylinder unscrewed to disclose a thick layer of shock absorbing thermal insulation which cradled a removable, toughened glass phial in which experimental samples of new and unfamiliar agents would be routinely stored. In the top of the lid was a small valve. When the contents were particularly unpleasant, or the TCR was being transported on public roads, the air could be withdrawn from the interior creating a partial vacuum which reinforced the seal of the lid, and ensured that any molecular seepage would be inwards rather than outwards. The valve also allowed for a sample of the interior air to be taken if the cylinder had suffered any physical insult which might have damaged the contents.

Next to the valve, in the centre of the lid, was a protruding, pierced lug through which a key-ring was fitted. Attached to the ring there would normally be a small steel cylinder of the type sometimes found on the collars of dogs. This held a roll of paper on which details of the contents of the phial would be written, along with information regarding any antidotes or treatments, the licensee responsible for the product, its laboratory of origin and, where appropriate, its destination. On the TCR in Duncan's hand, however, this cylinder had been removed and replaced with a plastic tag engraved with a large number six.

"Earlier this morning I took five TCRs; the one holding the Teronin, and four containing phials of an innocuous liquid. I gave each a tag like this with a number from one to five. Sir Graham then changed the numbers round. At this point neither of us, nor anyone else, knows which one holds the T2.

"All five will remain in the strong room until Tuesday night, when five unmarked police cars will arrive here, each with a driver and an armed escort. The cars will leave at random intervals, travel by different routes, and keep in touch via police control. No-one could hope to track and attack all five vehicles, and with only a twenty per cent chance of success it will not be worth their while to go for one of them.

"Once all five TCRs are safely aboard the *Lysander* I shall call Sir Graham, who will tell me how he changed the numbers, and I can then place the real T2 in safe keeping on the ship. He looked round at the three faces. "And I want you to come with me."

"Us? What on earth for?" It was Anthony Goodyear, but from their faces he spoke for all three.

"Two reasons. Firstly you are the only people who know what we're carrying, and if there are any problems I would like you on hand."

"If there are any problems with that stuff you won't want a scientist, you'll want a priest."

"And I don't know any more about it than you do," objected Charlie Wilson. "I'm a physicist, not a chemist."

"I know, but you know what we're dealing with. If a problem arose you wouldn't need convincing of the seriousness of the situation, or what the stakes are."

Miles Roper looked at him dubiously. "What was your second reason?"

Duncan looked him straight in the eye. "Two men have already been killed; I don't want any more. If I was a member of the opposition and I had failed to get what I wanted from Skinner and Dobbs my next port of call would almost certainly be one of the section heads. Until the T2 is safely on Johnston Atoll I can't think of anywhere safer for the three of you than on a fully armed warship surrounded by members of Her Majesty's Navy."

A *frisson* went round the group. "You think we are at risk?"

"It's a possibility we have to face."

"Then what about Graham? You didn't mention him."

"Yes, Sir Graham may be in danger too, but someone has to stay here and run things. And I am making arrangements for his protection."

Miles Roper took out his pipe and sucked on it. It was empty, and would remain so until after the evening meal when he would have his one and only smoke of the day, but it spent more time in his mouth than out. "How long will this trip take?"

"Not long. There's an airport on Johnston. Once delivery has safely taken place we'll fly you back. Say three weeks at the most."

"Three weeks!" Anthony Goodyear looked apoplectic. "The field trials of my ultra-low-frequency anti-personnel system start a week tomorrow."

"I'm sure Guy Talbot can cope. And I'll be on tap." Huish did not make it sound as though the point was open to discussion. "And you won't be out of touch, Tony. We'll keep you informed how they're going."

Roper sucked noisily on his pipe. "So. A week to prepare then. I too have things on the boil; I better get to it. Was there anything else?"

"Yes, one final thing." Duncan had been prepared to apply pressure, and was pleased that he had got his way with such relative ease. "I have arranged for the Highlanders to hold manoeuvres here for the next couple of weeks. It'll help with security. I have told their C.O. that we have seen prowlers round the perimeter fence, so his men will be on the lookout. It'll be a useful addition to our own staff.

"I think that about ties things up. Are there any questions?"

"I'm sure I shall think of some, but we know where to find you." Charlie Wilson rose to his feet. "Well I better go and prepare my lab for my absence."

The others took their cue and headed back to their offices and laboratories, debating what explanation to give their staff for their forthcoming, abrupt departure.

...

The Perimeter fence around Lairig a' Mhuic is positioned so that at no point is the complex it protects visible from the outside. The fence therefore encloses a great deal more of Scotland than the few dozen acres of the development itself, and to put this surplus, secure land to maximum use the scientists are from time to time joined by various branches of the armed forces who move in and practice some of their more esoteric exercises among the hills on the opposite side of the lake.

It was thus not a total surprise for Rory Kilbride to find on arrival at work that he had to join the tail end of a convoy of the Queen's Own Highlanders being checked through the gates, though it was odd that he had not been given the usual warning.

He waited while the last three trucks were passed through by the reception committee of Duncan McLennan, Hamish Fraser, and the

Highlanders' Commanding Officer, Colonel McCrae, and when it was his turn he handed Duncan his keys. "You never mentioned this lot," he told his superior, a trace of admonition in his voice.

"Last minute decision," Duncan replied evenly. "They were supposed to have cleared it a month ago, but somebody blundered. Col. McCrae phoned last night, and I okayed it to get him out of a tight spot."

"I see." Rory accepted his keys back. "How long are they staying?"

"Couple of weeks or so." He waved Rory through.

An hour later, after Rory had had a swim, a shower and breakfast, they met again as he came on duty, and Duncan called him and Terry Davidson to his office. He looked tired and strained. "There are five shipments of decommissioned material going to Aberdeen next Tuesday night, and I shall be asking for volunteers to escort them. They are being shipped to the Johnston Island incinerator, and Dr. Goodyear will be going with them. The Yanks are having a problem with it and he is going to help them sort it out." He made no mention of Miles Roper or M.M. "I am escorting him, and I should like one of you to accompany me."

There was no question of whether either would volunteer; as Duncan knew they would both jump at the chance. It was Terry who answered with a grin: "Better toss for it, I suppose?" He looked at Rory who nodded his agreement.

Terry produced a coin and as he flipped it Rory called 'tails'. It came down heads.

"Right. Terry will come with me, you'll hold the fort here with Ben." Rory hid his disappointment. "We leave on Tuesday, and we'll be away about three weeks. Oh, and I want four other volunteers to come to Aberdeen for the first leg of the journey. Could you circulate the staff?"

The two agreed and left. As Rory returned to work it occurred to him that five shipments in one day was unusual. At six warheads to a lorry, that was a lot of material, and he was surprised that they had that much in store. In fact he would have sworn they didn't. This was not, after all, a factory; bulk manufacture went on elsewhere.

Two things happened during the course of the morning which disturbed Rory. Firstly he met Iain Hewitt, one of the visiting Highlanders whom he knew from a previous visit. During their conversation Iain casually referred to the problem of prowlers at the perimeter fence. When Rory pressed him for details he said that his C.O. had been asked by Mr. McLennan if he could alert his men to keep an eye open and be ready to react if there should be an attempted break-in. Rory said nothing to Iain, but he knew of no prowlers.

He might have dismissed this, had it not been for his lunch with Dr. Roper. This dapper little man, small and bald with bright, beady, intense eyes behind round, steel-rimmed spectacles, possessed like all the boffins of a telephone number IQ, seemed the most unlikely football fan, but when Rory had discovered he was a keen Dundee United supporter they had become immediate friends.

As usual they were discussing the fortunes of their team, but today he was not himself. Of course it was to be expected that he should be distracted - the deaths of his colleagues had put the whole community in a state of shock - but it was more than that; he seemed nervous, scared even, and evasive. And he also let it drop, hesitantly, as though he was uncertain whether he was free to talk about it, that he would be going away for two or three weeks, and so would Dr.Wilson and Dr. Goodyear. Rory told him he knew Goodyear was going, but not the others. Roper said defensively there was a conference they both wanted to attend.

It was not Rory's place to challenge that explanation, but an hour later he sought out Duncan and asked him what was going on.

"What do you mean?" was the guarded response. "What I say," Rory persisted. "There's something going on here which we're not being told about."

"Like what?"

"If I knew that I wouldn't be asking, but there are too many things happening all at once for them not to be connected. First there is a double suicide. Whatever reason did Dr. Skinner and Dr. Dobbs have for killing themselves? Haven't you wondered that?"

"I have, and there are any number of possible explanations: illness, debts, depression, some scandal we are yet to hear about.... Who, understands the working of the human mind?"

"Okay, though nobody here is aware of any problems. But then we have the army turning up overnight."

"I've told you about that."

"Yes, but you didn't tell me you were asking them to be prepared for a break-in."

McLennan raised his eyebrows. "Who told you that?"

"One of the Highlanders. He's a friend of mine."

"I see. Well perhaps Col. McCrae told them that to keep them on their toes."

"Are you telling me you didn't say it?"

"Listen Rory. I don't know why you're getting so excited just because the Highlanders turned up unexpectedly."

"That is not all. You then want *five* volunteers for escort duty next Tuesday, and all three section heads are going away on Tuesday as well."

"Yes. So I gather."

"And you're telling me all these things aren't connected?"

Duncan rubbed his hand across his eyes. He looked tired. "Look Rory, I don't need this. Yesterday I discovered the remains of two men whom I counted as friends. I have been up all night checking the security implications of their deaths and generally sorting their affairs, and now you are giving me the third degree.

"Apart from their sad demise I know of nothing you should be concerned about, so please go back to your work, and let me get on with mine."

It was out of character for Duncan to speak to him like this, and Rory was far from convinced. But he had been dismissed, and satisfied or not he had to go. He walked down to the jetty where the sailboards and dinghies were moored, thinking over his senior's response.

If it was anyone but Duncan giving him the brush off he would not take it lying down. But there were three men in the world he trusted unconditionally - his father, his grandfather, and Duncan. If he had thought about it he would have had to admit that he came close to loving Duncan as he did the other two.

He first met him when he joined the police force after leaving school, and Duncan was his Chief Inspector. Rory quickly grew to respect him for his fairness and honesty. No-one under C.I.

McLennan's command took shortcuts with the law, or helped cases along with a little enhancing of the evidence. Not that he was soft on criminals; he worked assiduously to bring to justice all transgressors, regardless of their station in life.

He was not a large man as policemen go. He was between 5'10" and 5'11", and was neither thick set nor slender. His fine, light brown hair was cut short enough to stop it falling over a face which perfectly reflected its owner's personality. It was a clear, open, honest face with regular features, some wrinkles, and a couple of small scars. A face with which one felt instinctively at home. If it hadn't been a face it would have been someone's favourite old sports jacket.

Although he had only been in the police force two years when Duncan left to take up the post at Lairig a' Mhuic, Rory decided to follow him when the Senior's post became available, as much for the sake of the man as the job.

And he had never regretted it.

He picked up a stone and tossed it into the water. He was still convinced that there was something up, but if Duncan said it was nothing for him to be concerned about, he supposed he would have to accept that.

CHAPTER 3

Andy Flynn paused for effect and looked round the hall. This was the climax of his speech, and it had his youthful, devoted audience's undivided attention. There were nearer forty than thirty people in the room. Not bad.

He looked again at Hannah Gentle. The photograph Gordon Carpenter had shown him did not do her justice. She was prettier; her face more alert and vivacious. It was strange to think that so much depended on that attractive teenager. He hoped she would not have to be hurt....

"So, to sum up," he returned to his script, "what evidence is there that the world has any understanding of the seriousness of the situation? A summit in Rio? A conference in Cairo? A handful of accords and protocols? Promises to reduce carbon dioxide emissions by a few percentage points? A few half-hearted recycling projects? It is like building a wall of matchboxes in the path of an avalanche. The Earth has been forming and evolving into an abundant, self-sustaining biosphere for 4,600 million years, and in the last two hundred - less than the blinking of an eye in biological time - it has been plundered and polluted to the point of extinction. Every year 300,000 tonnes of sulphur falls in the rain on Sweden alone, 7,300 million cubic meters of sewage and other waste are discharged into the North Sea. Every year 170,000 square kilometres of rain forest disappear, or to put it another way, the area of twenty football pitches every minute! At this rate it will all be gone in less than eighty years. And the equally important boreal forests are vanishing even more quickly. So the Earth loses its primary CO_2 scrubber.

"Meanwhile, every minute of every day we pump 40,000 tons of carbon dioxide into the atmosphere - increasing it's total volume by 25 per cent in the last hundred years. As you know, CO_2 raises the Earth's temperature, which leads to melting of the ice caps. But the white ice caps reflect sunlight back into space, while the dark oceans absorb it, and warm up. So as the polar caps shrink there is more ocean to warm the atmosphere, and less ice to cool it, and, to make things worse, large quantities of water vapour, itself a powerful greenhouse gas, are added

49

to the problem. So the planet gets warmer, more ice melts, and the cycle feeds on itself in an uncontrollable spiral.

"But, of course, that is not the end of the story. As the ice melts, water levels rise around the globe, and low lying land, which is usually the most fertile and productive, is lost. So we have less land to feed people, who are increasingly crammed together. And don't think I am talking about a few South Pacific islanders: if the ice caps melt altogether, which is by no means impossible, virtually all the world's major cities and most productive agricultural land will be lost beneath the sea.

"So while the number of people in the world rises by more than the population of Southampton every day, the land available to feed them shrinks, and what is left is less fertile. Bad farming practices, deforestation and climate change all cause soil erosion. Seventy-five billion tons of topsoil lost each year, while deserts expand at the rate of 60,000 square kilometres at a global cost of £270 billion. And it is the best soil, the top layers with most of the nutrients, that goes first. And where does it go? Into the rivers, which then flood and damage yet more arable land. In 1993 the Mississippi and the Missouri both flooded, causing $20bn worth of damage to crops and farms. There are no figures for similar damage in third world countries.

"We don't need a few token projects; the only thing that could - might - save the planet now would be wholesale, drastic changes of policy worldwide.

"Is this about to happen? I see no evidence of it. I see governments spending 1000 billion dollars each year on arms, but only a tiny fraction of that amount of environmental projects. I see people everywhere, no matter how much or how little they already have, clamouring for more and more energy-guzzling consumer goods. Who is going to tell them they can no longer have them? Their cars, their washing machines, their fridges, freezers, dishwashers, televisions, glossy magazines, daily newspapers, imported foodstuffs: the entire quick-frozen, disposable, pre-wrapped, centrally-heated, electrically operated lifestyle to which they feel they have an inalienable right, if only in the aspiration? Who is going to persuade them they must adopt what they see as the bleak and intolerable existence of an infinitely sustainable level of consumption?

"We try. As an organisation and as individuals we are all trying to educate people. But as H.G.Wells said, history is 'a race between education and catastrophe'. Think about it for a minute. Education is a slow, laborious process. Catastrophe is swift and merciless. It is, and always has been, an unequal race."

Flynn acknowledged the polite if tentative applause with a smile. He might be preaching to the converted, but he still enjoyed the effect this speech had on his audiences.

When the clapping died down he invited questions. There was the usual hiatus as everyone waited for someone else to break the silence, then an earnest-looking youth in the front row, with a pony tail and a cardigan which reached his knees, raised his hand.

"You paint a very bleak picture, Dr. Flynn. What is your answer?"

Flynn smiled politely. "I am a bio-physicist not a politician. I merely discover the facts and report them."

"But there must be an answer..."

"Must there?"

There was another uncomfortable silence, which was finally broken by another questioner.

"If things are as bad as you say, and we have passed the point of no return, there doesn't seem much point trying to do anything about it."

"That is a point of view, M..." Flynn bit off the word. 'Miss Gentle' he had been about to say - that would have taken some explaining! "Maybe that is the sad truth," he corrected himself.

"But then there's no hope?"

"On the contrary, I beg to differ. I would suggest that there is far too much hope. That it is the triumph of hope over experience that enables people to turn a blind eye to such an obvious and immediate catastrophe."

"So what are you saying? That there is no... no chance for the future?"

"I am saying nothing. I am merely giving you the facts as I know them. You must decide what those facts indicate."

It was a very thoughtful Hannah who left the meeting. She did not want to go for a drink with the others, and decided to walk home. She wanted to be alone to think.

She did not like Dr. Flynn. He was a poseur. He had enjoyed talking about those awful things. But she did not dispute his facts and figures - apart from anything else she had heard them all before; it was just that no-one before had put them all together so uncompromisingly, or spelled out so clearly what they meant.

She was so deep in thought that she nearly walked into the man on the street corner, peering equally intently at his map. He was tall, with a fresh, open look which she associated with Scandinavia, with sandy hair, and the short trousers of a holiday maker. As she apologised for her inattention he smiled and addressed her in broken English.

"Excuse me. You can help me perhaps? I lose myself."

She shared the smile with him. "Where are you trying to get to?"

"I seek the hotel Connaught on the street Huntingdon."

Hannah didn't know either, but she bent over his map and began to get her bearings. She found the university, and was tracing her way back to her flat when something sharp stabbed her painfully in the ribs.

"Get in the car." All trace of the accent had disappeared.

In its formative years the species Homo sapiens experienced stress in direct and immediate ways, typically in confrontation with wild animals. Such a situation allowed for one of only two responses: the victim could either do battle, or run away. Over the millennia the process of evolution endowed our ancestors with sophisticated and effective mechanisms to do this, which modern living rarely exploits. The fight/flight response is useless against the threat of an overdue mortgage, a constantly ringing telephone, or a nagging spouse, but when a life-threatening situation does arise the evolutionary package is as good as ever. From the moment the threat was made Hannah's adrenalin began to pump, and all unnecessary bodily functions ceased, while the vital ones were stimulated. Her digestive system closed down, and the blood which had been flowing to her stomach was redirected to the muscles and the brain. The capillaries in the skin closed - creating a sense of the blood 'running cold' - making yet more blood available to the brain and reducing the risk of bleeding should she be wounded.

With the available blood and oxygen directed to the muscles and the brain, her heart, similarly energised, began to pump it round harder and faster.

Stimulated by this sudden rush of oxygen- and hormone-enriched blood to the head, her brain was booted out of its quiet introspection, and began processing millions of bytes of information a second. In an almost infinitesimally short period of time she summed up the situation, and made a series of calculations based on her assessment.

Her assailant did not intend to kill her. If that was what he wanted he could have slipped the knife between her ribs, climbed into the car, and made his escape before anyone noticed her fall to the ground. The fact that he wanted her in the car meant that for the present at least he wanted her alive. Whether he was or was not prepared to kill her if she resisted she could not know, but what she did know, for an absolute certainty, was that if she once allowed him to get her into that car all chance of resistance would be gone, and whatever he and his colleagues had in mind for her they would be able to carry out with impunity. Her chance - her only chance - was now, and knife or no knife she had to take it.

Of the fight or flight options the latter was precluded by the hand that gripped her upper arm, yet landing an attack on an opponent six inches taller and many pounds heavier, who had a firm hold of her and a knife in her ribs, was no easy matter. In the next couple of microseconds she reviewed those options that did exist and made her selection.

The grip on her arm was intended to stop her running away, so grasping the element of surprise she used it to swing herself round and up towards her assailant where, when her face was as close to his as she could reach, she opened her mouth and began to scream.

She put everything she had into that scream. Every ounce of pent-up fear and fury, every available centilitre of lung capacity, every contortion of her vocal chords went into producing a note as high and loud and chilling as she could create.

And the effect was all she could have hoped for. Her attacker, who expected his knife to control the situation, was totally thrown. Having planned to spirit his quarry swiftly and silently from the streets of Perth, he now found himself clasping a seven stone banshee whose high decibel output was not only disorientating him physically and mentally, but drawing to the two of them the undivided attention of everyone from there to Dundee.

He had to hit her. It was the only thing; but both his hands were full. Instinctively he dropped the knife. It was useless anyway, a bluff; his instructions were not to harm her. He pulled back, pushing her away to take a swing, but as he did so Hannah's right knee shot up towards his groin. It might have settled matters had his reactions been slower, but once she changed her attack from the vocal to the physical she was moving into his territory, and sensing her body movement he side-stepped the approaching knee, moved forward, past Hannah, and grasping the front of her shirt tipped her effortlessly over his hip in a classic judo *osoto gari*.

The contest was over. Not exactly according to plan, but Hannah was overpowered. She felt her arm being twisted up her back and she was propelled up and forward into the waiting car. As her kidnapper piled in after her the man in the passenger seat leapt out and retrieved the fallen knife, and then the car shot off in a squeal of rubber and recrimination. It seemed the three non-combatants were unimpressed by their colleague's efforts, and were not hesitant to say so.

Hannah, for her part, crushed between two of them, looked frantically out for assistance. Her abduction had certainly not gone unnoticed. There were few people about, but those that were stood motionless, helplessly watching the departing car. Hannah twisted round to see out of the back window, praying for a miracle: a police car - a lone hero in crusading pursuit, his car phone to his ear as he reported the situation to the police...

There was nothing. The road behind was empty - not a vehicle in sight. As the full horror of her situation hit home a feeling of nausea and panic welled up inside her. Who were these men? What could they possibly want? Surely it was a case of mistaken identity; they had taken the wrong person. But would she be able to convince them? Fear and disbelief crawled in her stomach in equal proportions.

And then she saw her.

An elderly woman who had witnessed the struggle was peering at the car and writing the number on the back of her hand. And there was something else - a phone box. She was only a few yards from a phone box!

Hope replaced despair as Hannah began calculating. The woman runs to the box and dials 999. She would be speaking to the police within sixty seconds. Another minute and a call would go out giving the description and direction of the car. So three minutes and every police vehicle in Perth would be after them.

This was more than an outside chance, a wild dream. The odds were on her side. An image flooded into her mind of police cars from miles around homing in at high speed, talking to each other on their radios as they converged on the path of the big, black car, who's very speed made it conspicuous. For a moment she closed her eyes and offered up a silent prayer of gratitude to the woman in the brown coat who's quick thinking had alerted her rescuers, and called in the dark-blue cavalry of the Grampian Constabulary to her assistance.

Hope turned to consternation in less than a mile, however, as the car turned right and simultaneously halved its speed. Hannah now found herself cruising legally and anonymously through side streets at a steady thirty miles an hour. There were few pedestrians here, and she stared at each one they passed, frantically willing them to turn and read the fear in her eyes. But with the exception of one small boy who stopped pedalling his trike to look up and admire the big, black, shiny car as it slid past, not a soul paid them the slightest attention.

Giving up on telepathy Hannah hit once more on the idea of a vocal appeal for assistance. The windows were up in the back of the car, but the driver's was half way down, and a good scream should be clearly audible from outside. All she needed was the right person to hear it. She knew she would only get one chance, and there was no point screaming at children on bikes, or people on foot. What she needed was someone ....

What she needed was a platoon of off-duty commandos in a fast car! The sense of fear began to sink chillingly down through her until she had to make a conscious effort to control her bodily functions.

She was concentrating on this effort when, a short way ahead, she caught sight of something - or rather someone - which quickened her already racing pulse. He was a giant of a man, six feet six if he was an inch, with a body that might have been built of girder ends left over from the Forth bridge. He had a week's growth of beard; oily jeans that had been torn and patched and torn again, and he wore a black singlet several sizes too small which served to emphasise, as was no doubt intended, the muscles of the torso beneath. Over his shoulder was slung a massive padlock and chain, and he was about to swing his leg over a powerful motorcycle. Even in a poor light it would be hard to mistake him for a knight in shining armour, but Hannah knew he was the nearest thing to the young Lochinvar that she was likely to come across. She filled her lungs, and once again began to scream.

The man on her right swore and clapped his hand across her mouth, gripping her painfully by the cheeks. She tried without avail to bite the hand, unable to sink her teeth into the flat of the palm, but she was almost certain the man's head had turned towards them as he passed from her view. The driver, who had swerved when the sudden sound assailed his left ear, now glanced in his mirror and asked the colleague beside him: "Did he hear it?"

The co-pilot swivelled in his seat to look out of the back window. "I don't know, but I think probably yes." The driver said nothing but replied by pressing his foot to the floor. The large, powerful car leapt forward, sprinted to the end of the road, turned right, accelerated through another six hundred yards, and made a rapid left. The driver slowed again to a legal cruising speed, and all four passengers twisted round to peer behind them. The driver looked intently in his mirror.

The question was answered in seconds as the motorcycle appeared at speed, came to a skidding halt at the end of the road, and the rider turned towards them. Any lingering doubts they might have had when were dispelled when he heeled the bike over, gunned the engine, and the front wheel left the ground as he accelerated towards them. Hannah's whole body responded to this change of fortune. Hope and excitement and fear flooded through her in a confusing jumble.

As soon as the intentions of the pursuer were clear the driver of the car responded by once again putting his own vehicle through its paces. A large saloon car is no match for a powerful motorbike, but this Mercedes had something special under its bonnet. By the end of the road it was holding its own, and possibly even pulling away from its pursuer. The driver turned right with all the skill of a professional, using opposite lock to control their skid, and using the power of the engine to push the centre of gravity forward. Even so a ton and a quarter of steel on four wheels cannot turn through ninety degrees as quickly as a well-handled two-wheeler, and the motorbike gained on them on the turn. Again the car used its massive, turbocharged power plant to pull away down the straight, but again lost the initiative at the end of the road where a T junction demanded another sudden change of direction.

And the new road was full of traffic, which the bike could weave through and the car could not.

Hannah would not have believed she could have felt more scared than she already was, but when the driver pulled over onto the wrong side of the road into the path of an on-coming lorry, she thought she was going to be sick. She was pressed back into her seat as the car leapt towards the lorry, and she could see the startled driver's face as he stamped on the air brakes in a desperate attempt to avoid a head-on collision. They were only feet from his huge front bumper when the Mercedes heeled round into a side street on their right.

They accelerated down this street, leaving the lorry driver cursing, his hand on his horn, took the first left, and almost immediately left again down a narrow passage between two houses. At the end they pulled into a large double garage beside a Transit van, and as the driver switched off the engine Hannah could hear the sound of a powerful motorcycle roar past the end of the entrance. She felt very close to tears.

Once the doors had been shut behind them a light was switched on, and Hannah was escorted out of the car. The reception committee of two who were waiting for them looked Hannah up and down like customers taking delivery of a new car, checking it for damage.

"No problems?" grunted the taller of the two. It was half statement half question.

"Nothing I couldn't handle," replied her abductor defensively, "but she's got a hell of a mouth on her. Have you got that tape?"

The other went to the back of the Transit and returned with a roll of wide surgical tape. He cut off six inches and Hannah was held while it was placed over her mouth, and her hands were tied behind her back, and then her feet. Without more ado the larger of the two men lifted her into the back of the Transit, and the doors were closed behind them. Someone, Hannah assumed it to be the other of the two men who had been waiting for them, climbed into the driver's seat, and started the engine as the garage doors were opened again. The van drove slowly down the alleyway to the road, and, Hannah noticed with a heavy heart, turned right. Any hopes she had of rescue were completely gone. All those police cars she had imagined speeding to her rescue would be looking for a black car heading East, while she was in the back of a battered blue van driving slowly West.

She examined her surroundings. The rear windows of the vehicle had been crudely boarded over with pieces of paint-spattered plywood, sufficiently ill-fitting to allow in enough light to see by - not that that there was much to look at. There was a bulkhead between their compartment and the driver, and up against this, facing backwards, a car seat had been spot-welded to the floor. Her escort sat on this in an uncompanionable silence, and apart from him the van was quite empty. Hannah lay on the floor on her side, the only concession to her comfort being a grubby piece of mat that someone had thrown across the uneven metal. With her hands tied behind her back there was no position in which she could lie comfortably, and unable to brace herself against the movement of the vehicle every action of braking and accelerating and turning, and every bump in the road, added to her discomfort.

But what troubled her more than her physical distress were the twin unanswerable questions: why had she been kidnapped, and where was she being taken? At first she tried to follow the changes of direction taken by the van and commit them to memory, but it was almost impossible in that confined, darkened box to tell a left turn from a right, and anyway, as they threaded their way though side streets, she very quickly lost track. From then on the journey became one long, increasingly painful series of jolts and bumps and rolls. It was as difficult to judge their speed and the passage of time as it was their direction, but it became increasingly apparent that it was no short, local journey. The irritation of the itches she could not scratch and the aches she could not rub were in time joined by the demands of her bladder which increasingly required emptying. She arched her back and tried to look at her companion, but with her eyes level with his

58

feet she could barely see his face. She tried to get his attention by making grunting noises through her nose, but he was dozing, and the noise of the engine and the various rattles of the van overwhelmed her attempts. She curled her knees up further, and tried to distract herself by going again over the possible reasons for her abduction. The only thing she felt fairly sure of was that sex, as a motive, was out. Four men might jointly kidnap a woman for sexual purposes, but why then hand her over to others? She wasn't sure whether she was relieved or not. By any rational standard she should be, but what were the alternatives? The fact that she could not think of any made it more sinister.

And there was another thing. Something she had been half conscious of before, which now focussed itself intensely on her troubled mind.

Six men. She had seen six men. Clearly. Close up. She could identify each of them without the slightest difficulty, and yet not one of them had made any attempt to hide his identity. The more she thought about that, the more the implications terrified her, and the sense of terror did nothing to assist the state of her bladder. In the end the pain from that quarter came to override all else, and her battle not to allow herself to suffer the ignominy of enuresis took up every ounce of physical and emotional energy.

And the journey went on and on. In time the numbness in her hips and shoulders spread through the rest of her body, and she became enveloped in a cachectic semiconsciousness. Her tortured brain even began to ignore the messages from her bladder, and the sense of detachment released her mind from the worst of the torments of her body. Time ceased to have any meaning.

She could not have judged to a couple of hours how long they had been travelling when she first became aware that their progress had changed. They must have left the main roads behind, for now they were weaving their way slowly along winding lanes. Twice they had to stop and back, and Hannah heard the growl of a tractor crawling carefully past the van, inches from her head; only a flimsy sheet of steel between her and the driver. The sense of help so close, yet so infinitely unreachable, stung her mind back to some sort of alertness, and the awareness that they must be nearing the end of their journey brought a mixture of relief and fear.

She began once again to wonder where she had been brought, and why, but the answers were no more obvious after hours of appalling discomfort than they had been before it. She was starting to dwell on some of the more disquieting possibilities when the van slowed again, made a sharp turn, and began crunching slowly up a gravel drive.

When the engine was finally switched off, Hannah strained for any sounds that might give a clue to her whereabouts, but her ears, still ringing from the hours of constant noise, picked up nothing. She twisted and lifted her head to look at her companion. He was slowly coming to, the stillness and silence waking him from an uncomfortable sleep and Hannah dropped her head again and awaited events.

The driver's door slammed, and she heard his feet scrunch across the gravel. She waited for what seemed an eternity as her senses returned to life, and with them pain, before a distant door slammed, and footsteps approached the van.

The padlock rattled, and as the doors were opened the dark interior was flooded with the flat, cold light of early morning. Two men climbed into the van, grunted a greeting to her yawning companion of the night, and unceremoniously lifted her out.

She was set down on her feet facing a tall, attractive man, probably in his early thirties, who could have stepped out of the pages of any magazine that advertised rugged outdoor clothing. The heavy, lumberjack's check shirt and blue jeans he was wearing hung on him with the effortless elegance that so few men are able to attain. He studied her with interest and the hint of a smile.

"Was the sticking plaster entirely necessary?" he asked the driver.

"Yeah. She's a screamer."

"Is she?" Her host's smile was untroubled. "Well I don't think we shall need it here." He looked theatrically around him, and Hannah followed suit. They were in a large country garden, and although the longer view was mostly obscured by by trees and hedges, where there were gaps she could see only open countryside beyond. "We are more than two miles from the next inhabited building," he said, turning back to Hannah. "If you take it to extremes I suppose we might have to replace the plaster for the sake of our own peace and quiet, but if you feel so inclined you may scream as loudly as you like." He nodded to one of his henchmen, and while the tape was being peeled from Hannah's face he continued in the same conversational vein. "You will forgive my not making formal introductions, but you may call me 'John'. Assuming you behave yourself you will come to no immediate harm. You will, however, be staying with us for some little while, so I suggest you try to make the most of it."

Hannah, now free to speak, made a great effort to put as much false confidence into her voice as she could muster. "I need the toilet," she said bluntly.

"Of course you do. How thoughtless of me. Carl, show Miss Gentle to her quarters." He turned back to his captive. "I shall give you a chance to settle in, and then I shall be pleased to answer any questions you may have."

Hannah's feet and hands were untied and Carl and her other escort led her away into the house. It was a large, stone building, of indeterminate age, but old enough to have had several additions and modifications in its lifetime as various owners had adapted it to their own individual whims. Hannah was led through an imposing panelled hall where a handful of threadbare and mournful animal heads peered down upon her passage, and through an equally capacious kitchen into what would originally have been the scullery, and was now a utility room. Here the one called Carl, who was a great hirsute lump of a man with thick bristly hair everywhere and a lumbering gait that was a cross between a swagger and a stagger, produced a bunch of keys from his pocket. He opened a door in the corner of the room, and led the way down a flight of steps into the cellar.

Hannah, her other escort on her heels, followed him down into a vaulted, cavernous room. An assortment of household jumble, from empty tea chests to dead refrigerators, stood in neglected disarray between the wine racks which lined the walls. From here they went through an archway into a second, slightly smaller chamber where only an old bicycle and some ancient horse bridles collected cobwebs, and beyond that into a third. This last room was as large as the first, though longer and narrower, and a few feet in, across its entire width, steel bars had been installed, converting the far end into a prison cell. Carl, who still had his keys in his hand, opened the door in the bars, and stood aside to let Hannah enter.

As prisons go it could have been worse, and some attempt had been made to make it as comfortable as possible under the circumstances. There was a bed, with a couple of soft-looking pillows and a duvet in a cheerful, white and yellow print cover; an old fashioned wash stand with a china bowl on top and matching jug of water underneath; an armchair; a table with a small television, radio and selection of books and magazines; and, most welcoming of all, in a curtained off corner, a portable toilet. Hannah hurried over to it, as Carl closed and locked her cell door.

Twenty minutes later, as she was completing an inspection of the accommodation, the man calling himself John appeared.

"I trust you can make yourself reasonably comfortable here, Miss Gentle. I regret we could not arrange running water, but you will appreciate the drainage is a problem in a cellar. However we shall keep you furnished with a fresh supply as and when you need it, and you will be allowed to use the bathroom upstairs on a supervised basis. You will, as long as you behave yourself, also be allowed regular exercise in the grounds.

"As for the rest, you have control of your own lighting and heating. I shall try to accommodate any reasonable requests regarding food or reading materials or toiletries.

"One thing I would draw your attention to is this." He pointed above his head to a small, wall-mounted video camera. "It is, you understand, just for our peace of mind. You may, of course, dress and undress behind the curtain."

He gave her a smile which appeared to betray a mixture of genuine warmth and apology. "I'm not sure that I will answer them all, but do you have any questions?"

• • •

At 03.00 Rory set out on a routine tour of inspection. Many of his colleagues made these tours as quickly as possible, running round the various check points in their cars, anxious to get back to the warmth of the office, the coffee maker and the TV.

Rory, however, preferred to walk if the weather was half-way decent. He enjoyed the exercise, and the sights and sounds of the night. He knew of two tawny owl's nests, one down by the incinerator, the other just below the apartments, and on the hill, nearer the tarn, was a badgers' sett. Sometimes on a moonlit night he would stand in the shade of the school room and watch them going about their business.

Tonight as he walked up towards the residential area he saw a pair of hedgehogs, but no badgers. Perhaps they were using their other entrance in the wood, further off to his right. As he reached the top of the hill a rabbit who was sitting in the middle of the road darted off, its white scut flashing a warning of the approaching human danger. But apart from that the area was deserted. He walked up the cul-de-sac to his left past the houses of the senior personnel, and back again. He wandered down to the flats, round the small loop the road made at the end, and then turned left back down the hill on the service road which ran parallel with the main one he had walked up. More flats and small houses lined the left hand side of the road, but like the others they were still and quiet, and dark except for the occasional outside light which had been left on. In one a dog barked as Rory's shadow passed the glass panelled door of his owner's house; but otherwise Lairig a' Mhuic was asleep.

Down to his right a silvery golden line of light pointed across the surface of the tarn towards the moon, which hung large and bright in the cold morning sky. Directly ahead of him was the Recreation block, and beyond that, visible over its octagonal roof, the Administration building and the office where he had left Hammond Innes open at the end of a chapter.

He had also left the light on, and as he glanced casually towards his room he saw what looked for all the world like the shadow of a man - or woman - move across the lighted rectangle.

He stopped walking and stared. Of course there was no reason why someone should not be up and about. Some insomniac going for a walk. And where better to go for company than the night duty officer's

63

room, where the one person who was bound to be awake could be found?

Rory set back down the hill, repeating this explanation to himself. It was the obvious one; people did sometimes drop into the office when they couldn't sleep.

So why had he felt that strange chill when he saw the figure? Was it his imagination, or had it been moving furtively? After all he had been several hundred yards away.

But it had been an instinct, and one of the maxims Duncan had instilled into him in his earliest days as a rookie policeman was to trust his instincts. Or at the very least, not to ignore them.

At the bottom of the hill he left the roadway and forked off left around the northern corner of the school room. The Rec was now between him and his office, and he walked quietly between it and the swimming pool. As he emerged he stayed close to the wall of the Rec, moving slowly as more and more of the Administration block came into his field of view across the playing field.

At the next corner he stopped and stared towards his office. He could see nothing. Had the figure been inside his room or outside? He could not tell.

It was a clear, cold night with a slight ground frost. The sort of night in which every sound travels. He heard one of his owls call from over by the laboratories, but apart from that, nothing. All was silence.

Slowly he began to cross the playing field, keeping the football net between him and the lighted window. When he reached the goal post he stopped again and looked, but still he could see nothing. Moving on, more quickly now, he crossed the open ground to the chain link fence that isolated the laboratory complex. At the security check point, just across the road from the Administration building and the car park, he once again stopped and stared and listened, but still he could only hear the innocent and distant sounds of the night.

He stepped round the corner and made for the front door, keeping close to the gates on his left, and stopping to check the padlock he himself had put on at 23.30 when he locked up the labs. It was intact.

He did not enter the office; preferring to check the outside first. As silently as he could he made his way round the irregularly shaped building, crouching as he passed each window. The moonlight would cast a clear shadow into an unlit room, and he had no intention of advertising his presence in the way his quarry had done.

Only one room had a light burning, and that was the one he had left twenty minutes ago. If the figure he had seen was that of an innocent insomniac that is where they would be, sitting in the warm waiting for the night duty officer to return. Rory peeped in.

The room was empty, just as he had left it. The papers on his desk lay undisturbed, his book open, face down on his chair.

He continued his stealthy tour until he came to the point where the chain link fence adjoined the north-west wall, annexing part of the building within the security area. He did not examine the fence. If that had been tampered with the alarm would be ringing and the whole complex would be awake.

Satisfied that no-one was lurking outside in the darkness he made his way back to the front door. It was unlocked as he had left it; internal security depended on individuals locking the doors of their offices. He let himself in, turned on the corridor lights, and began walking round checking the doors. Most were locked, but whenever one gave he opened it, put on the lights, and checked the room.

On the ground floor Duncan's office and the Chief Admin Officer's were both locked, as were the small security post by the laboratory gates, the telephone exchange, and the cleaner's office and store room. The secretaries' office, the security teams' day room and locker room were open but empty.

Rory ascended the stairs, increasingly wondering whether he had not imagined the whole thing. Could it have been a trick of the light? An owl, closer to him than he realised and so looking as big as a man against the lighted window?

The first door he came to at the top of the stairs was that of Sir Graham Huish's office. Casually he tried the handle. It was locked, and he was about to move on when something caught his eye. Just below his hand were two parallel marks in the dark wood of the door frame. He crouched down and shone his torch on them, and saw that the wood was splintered. Something about an inch wide had been forced between the door and the frame just below the lock, and then levered. He stroked the edge of the door with his fingers and felt an indentation where the wood fibres had been compressed. Somebody had tried to force open the door.

That decided it. This warranted a full security alert. He unclipped the radio from his belt and put it to his ear, but as his thumb was about to depress the 'send' button something hard hit him on the back of the head and sent him sprawling on the floor. He had dropped his guard; let himself be distracted by the damaged lock, and momentarily ignored his own immediate safety.

And in that moment someone had stepped round the corner in stockinged feet and hit him on the head with the jemmy they had been using on the door. As Rory hit the floor he expected to pass out, but although his head hurt sickeningly and his eyes swam he remained conscious. He was aware of his radio lying on the floor a yard from his face, and of a curved blue wrecking bar in a gloved hand swinging down and smashing it, and of the unseen owner of the hand fleeing silently towards the stairs.

He could not have been hit very hard, he concluded, as he reached painfully round to feel the back of his head. Was that incompetence or compassion, he wondered. His hand came away sticky and red. It was not all that compassionate.

The only thing he had seen of his attacker was an inch of wrist. A man's wrist.

Well that narrows down the field, he thought wryly to himself.

Cautiously he tried to get up. The corridor was spinning and he felt violently sick. Using the wall for support he made it into an upright position, and stood there a while wondering whether he was going to fall over again.

When he found he could stand, albeit with assistance, he launched a brave experiment to see if he could move as well. His legs felt like jelly, and even the wall seemed to move unpredictably beneath his hand, but when he gave it his full concentration he found he was able, just, to propel himself along. It was like walking on a trampoline on the deck of a small boat in a rough sea, but if he stopped for the worst waves and troughs he could lurch forward a few paces between them.

He made it to the top of the stairs, where there was a handrail to help him. Grasping this with both hands he began his descent, and unsteadily lowered himself one tread at time down the six steps to the half way landing where the flight turned back on itself.

Here he stopped briefly, aware that he was starting to get the hang of things, and that his head, though still aching, was beginning to clear. He let go of the handrail, and crossed to the one opposite in a controlled lurch. As he grabbed it, pleased with his five unsupported steps, he heard a bang below him, and realised the front door had just slammed shut. His attacker had only just left the building, having stopped to replace the shoes he had removed to creep up on Rory.

Galvanised by this realisation Rory launched himself without a thought at the second flight of stairs and went down them at a trot. With the help of the handrail he made it to the bottom where he abandoned all caution and set off for the front door at a loping sprint. Once through it the cold air hit him, and his head cleared perceptibly.

His attacker obviously had to be someone from within the perimeter fence. Of course that now included the Highlanders, but he could not see why one of them would be interested in Sir Graham's office. Therefore it was someone from Lairig, in which case they would now most likely be heading back towards the living quarters up the hill opposite him.

But the bank was bathed in moonlight, and anyone going up it would be clearly visible. Which implied they were either hiding behind the Rec or the swimming pool, or they had gone the other way. That way they could cut across to the stores and workshops from where they could work their way back to their flat or house either by going round the far side of the tarn, or round the laboratories and through the wood.

Rory turned and ran across the car park and round the side of the building where, a hundred and fifty yards away, he could see the dark shapes of the stores, workshops and garage. And to the right, another moving shape was just in the process of merging into their shadows.

Rory set off, running now swiftly and confidently despite the pain that hammered in his head each time a foot hit the ground, and the blood that was running down the back of his neck and soaking into his shirt. But he was fit and in condition, and he crossed the open space in a very respectable time.

As he reached the point where the fleeing figure had disappeared, he stopped, and gave his eyes a chance to adjust to the darkness.

Coming out of the brightly lit building his night vision was gone, and he could not afford to go blundering blindly after a man with a weapon. As his eyes acclimatised themselves he began to creep slowly forward along the wall of the stores building, ahead of him the silhouettes of the pumps where Lairig's vehicles refuelled.

When he drew level with the door he tried the handle, but it was locked. He continued to the far corner of the building, and peered round.

The grass here gave way to concrete which formed the large hard standing which surrounded the garage opposite him, its three roller doors closed as far as he could tell. The scene was a mosaic of bright concrete and dark, impenetrable shadows thrown by the buildings and the various vehicles that stood about. Rory identified the bin lorry, the gritting lorry and the tow truck, and the fire engine which stood in its own garage at the edge of the concrete.

He stared at each of these in turn, trying to divine any movement. Or a shadow within a shadow. There were a dozen places a man could hide, but he could detect nothing in any of them.

To go further meant crossing a patch of moonlight, when he would be clearly visible to anyone watching, but his quarry might already be making his way round the laboratories, and he could not stay put indefinitely. He doubled up and sprinted across to the shadow of the gritting lorry, flattened himself against the side of it, and waited to see if this action would cause any reaction.

There was none.

While he decided where to head next he cursed himself that he did not do the rounds by car like everyone else. He'd have been round the whole base in ten minutes, and caught the prowler red-handed, and even if he had got away he would not have had to give chase on foot.

And then a sobering thought struck him.

Supposing it was not a coincidence? What if the intruder knew Rory's habits. He could have deliberately waited for a night when he was on duty as the only chance he would have to be alone in the Admin building for any length of time. If Rory had not seen the man when he did, he would have continued on his rounds at a leisurely pace, checking the pool and filtration plant, the labs and the incinerator. He was normally out for a good forty minutes; often more if it was a nice night like tonight.

Why this seemed more shocking he could not say. He had already accepted it must be someone from Lairig, and he knew everybody there by sight at least. But the idea that his routine was an essential part of the break-in suddenly made it very personal.

More determined than ever to find out who had damaged Sir Graham's woodwork and his own head, he swung round the bonnet of the lorry and began running openly towards the garage.

Almost as he set out, however, he heard a noise from around the far end of the building. It was a grinding, mechanical sound which he recognised but could not quite place until an ancient engine leapt into life. Instinctively he ran towards it, but as he did so the tractor's gears were gratingly engaged and the machine chugged round the corner to meet him. As it turned the driver switched on the headlights, catching Rory squarely in their beam. He stood there, dazzled, as they bore down on him from barely his own length away.

He dived to his right, rolling as he hit the ground but still causing flashing lights in his throbbing head and a sheet of pain which reached down to the soles of his feet.

Fearful that the tractor would turn and come back for another go at him he scrambled to pick himself up and began hobbling away. But there was no second attempt, and the machine continued on its way, intent only on escape. And then it dawned on him that the driver, swinging the machine round the corner, could not have know that Rory would be racing towards him. It had not been a deliberate attempt on his life.

He turned and began to give chase. It was the old Fordson, which many of them still felt was the best machine for general use. It was easy to drive, had a good turning circle, and was surprisingly reliable. But it was not fast. And, unless it been fixed in the last week, top gear would still not engage most of the time.

It was heading back down towards the Rec, and Rory ran hard after its one working tail light. The frosty ground made running difficult, and his shoes did not grip well. Several times he nearly fell, and he could not even approach his best speed. The tractor was steadily pulling ahead, but it was also angling across the grass towards

69

the metalled roadway. Rory made his angle even sharper: the sooner he was on a hard surface the sooner he could speed up.

He reached the road, and gulping great lungfuls of the cold, clear air he put on a spurt and watched the red light begin to get closer. He was gaining on the ancient, rumbling machine. Inspired by this success he cranked himself up yet another notch, and as the Fordson passed the Rec he was no more than fifteen yards behind.

By the schoolhouse it was down to ten, and in another thirty seconds he would have caught it. But then he hit the hill. The tractor, unaffected,lumbered on, but Rory's speed dropped significantly. Slowly but inexorably the gap began to widen. And to make matters worse they had left the road way and were once more on the grass. There was a great temptation to give up. To stop, and let his exhausted body recover. But he battled on. All he needed to do, after all, was identify the driver. So long as he could keep in touch....

The same thought must have occurred to the tractor driver at about the same time. Covering his face with his hand he twisted briefly round to check his pursuer's position, and then, as he reached the top of the hill, he swung the wheel violently round, turning the vehicle so quickly that two wheels momentarily left the ground. With his hand spread across his face he aimed the tractor directly at Rory, now some thirty yards away down the hill, and leapt off the back.

Rory stopped at last, transfixed for a second time by the oncoming lights of the tractor as it bounded towards him, its wheels steering themselves in response to the uneven ground. He watched its progress for a few seconds, gauging its general tendency to be a downhill arc, and as it was almost upon him he dived as far to his left as he could.

All other things being equal this should have taken him at least three feet clear of the runaway machine, but as he craned his head round to watch it pass he saw it lurch in the darkness as it hit a hump in the ground and slew round towards him. He was now lying directly in the path of its wheels. Instinctively he tried to roll away, but that involved rolling uphill, and gravity was against him. As the front wheel reached his foot he did the only thing he could; he rolled downhill, under the tractor.

He knew that if he moved too far he would be under the sump at the front and the differential at the back, either of which might catch him, so he deliberately stayed as close to the wheels as he dared. As the ancient machine thundered over him, the noise from its superannuated engine terrifying at such close range, the front wheel passed him with inches to spare. But the wider rear wheels, with their massive tyres, took up more space, and actually rubbed against him as they rolled. If he had been three inches further up the hill he would have been crushed, with almost certainly fatal results.

When the beast finally made it past him, Rory dropped his head to the ground. Dearly as he would have loved to stay there and indulge the overwhelming sense of exhaustion that had enveloped him, he forced himself up once more and peered up the hill. But his night sight had been destroyed again by the tractor's lights, and there was, he realised with chagrin, almost certainly nothing there to see. Whoever he had been following would have had plenty of time to scuttle off to their lair, and shut themselves safely in. By the time he reached the top of the hill they would probably be in bed.

Dejectedly Rory pulled himself to his feet and watched the Fordson career on down the hill and plunge into the tarn. Wearily and painfully he began to trudge towards Duncan's flat. The incident had to be reported immediately, regardless of the hour.

Rory was more than a little surprised when Duncan answered the door fully dressed.

"What are you doing up at this hour?" he asked him.

"Catching up on some work," Duncan answered easily. "And what are you doing calling at this hour?"

"I have come to report something."

Rory accepted an invitation to go in, and sat and told his story in the warm. Duncan went out with him to look at the Fordson, and they briefly examined the slope with their torches. The tyre tracks could be seen in the frost, but not the footprints. There was nothing to indicate who the tractor driver was, or where he had gone.

"And you are still saying there is nothing going on here?" Rory asked at last.

Duncan did not respond for a moment.

"No. I suppose that line does not hold up now, does it? So yes, there is something going on, and this is no doubt part of it. But I am not going to tell you any more. Not for the moment at least.

71

"Oh. And keep this to yourself. That's an order."

CHAPTER 4

Rory knew as he turned the key in his lock that Hannah had not come. Strange how the front door always betrays an empty home. Disappointed, he made himself a cup of tea, watched the news on television, then cooked an omelette.

By the time he had finished washing up and putting away the dishes it was clear she was not coming. Presumably she was stuck into her essay. He phoned Colin Coltrane and arranged to meet him at the bowling alley, where they played four games, drawing two all.

The next day there was a definite atmosphere at Lairig a' Mhuic. The two deaths were obviously part of it, but Rory suspected more than that. He detected an air of uncertainty, even distrust. He discovered he was not the only one to notice it, but no-one he spoke to could put a finger on it. Whatever was going on it was not conducive to a cheerful workplace, and for the first time he could remember he was relieved to leave work.

It was raining steadily, which annoyed him as it meant he could not have the top down on the car, and by the time he reached Luncarty he felt in need of cheering up. He went home first to see if Hannah was there, and when she wasn't decided he would treat her to a Chinese carry-out. He drove to her flat.

When she did not answer the door he let himself in with his key, cursing that she was not on the phone. He hated wasted journeys. He checked each room, and found nothing to indicate where she was, or when she might be home. It was odd in a way; he had expected to find pages of writing and reference books strewn around the floor and sofa, as they usually were when she was in the middle of a long essay. The place hardly looked as though she had been in it since he was there two nights ago. Even the two mugs they had used were still on the coffee table, unwashed.

He shrugged. Hannah was not as fastidious as he was about cleaning up, and it was not unheard of for her to spend a couple of nights with a girlfriend, dispensing sympathy in exchange for details.

But it was unusual for her not to phone Rory and tell him.

Not sure whether to be anxious or annoyed, he left a note asking her to ring him urgently, and returned home, collecting a meal for one.

He stayed in, not wanting to leave the phone, and watched TV.

By the following night he was decidedly worried. Again he checked his flat on the way past, then hurried on to Hannah's. The place was unchanged, and she had clearly not been in it for the past twenty-four hours. He tried a couple of the neighbours, but this was bed-sitter land, and although they knew Hannah to pass the time of day, neither knew anything of her whereabouts.

He went back into her flat, and found the note book in which she kept her telephone numbers. He put it in his pocket and returned home, not bothering about food.

Sitting by his phone with the notebook on his knee, he wondered whom to ring first. It was no good trying to contact the college, that would be shut now. And tomorrow was the weekend. He kicked himself for leaving it so late.

He wondered about phoning her parents, but she would surely have told him if she was going there, and it would only worry them. Which left her friends. He was going through the neatly written names when the phone at his elbow rang.

With a surge of relief, certain, for no good reason, that it would be her, he reached for the instrument and picked it up.

An unpleasant voice said: "She wasn't there, was she?"

"Who wasn't where?" Annoyed and disappointed that it wasn't Hannah, Rory was in no mood for riddles.

"Your young lady friend. You called on her at 6.41 and she wasn't there."

Something large and lumpy changed position in Rory's stomach. "Who is this?"

"That's because she's here with me." The question was ignored.

"Who the hell are you?" The receiver trembled in Rory's clenched fist as he fought to control the anger boiling up inside him.

"This is what I want you to do." The Voice was not good at answering questions. "When the Lysander sails, I want you to be on it."

Rory's head was spinning. He had no idea what the man was talking about. "Where's Hannah? What have you done with her?"

There was a menacing pause, and then The Voice said with strained patience: "I told you. She's here with me. Would you like to hear her scream?"

"No, don't hurt her." It occurred to Rory that he was dealing with a madman, and the hairs on his scalp bristled at the thought of what Hannah must be going through. "The Lysander," he said, trying to sound interested and appeasing. "I'm afraid I've never heard of it."

There was another, shorter pause.

"Are you having me on pal?"

"No, seriously, I..."

"And I suppose you don't know anything about a trip to Aberdeen on Tuesday?"

"Oh, I see. Yes. I just didn't know the ship was called the Lysander."

"Well it is, and I want you on it."

"But I can't do that. They've already decided who's going."

"Then you'd better undecide them. You are to be on the boat."

Rory's mind was racing. "I'll do whatever I can."

"No, pal. You'll make it happen. Unless you want very nasty things to happen to your young lady here."

"No, of course not." Rory took a calculated risk - for Hannah's sake he could not afford to antagonise this man. "Let me speak to her."

"No chance."

"Then how do I know you've got her?"

"She's missing, isn't she?"

"Yes. But I want to know she's alive and unharmed."

There was a grunt. "Hang on."

For thirty seconds Rory could hear nothing, the phone having been silenced in some way, and then The Voice returned. "She says to tell you 'blue remembered hills', whatever the hell those are when they are at home."

Rory winced. "Okay. I'll do it."

"And if you need any help - like nobbling anyone who's in the way or whatever - you ring this number." he gave Rory the number of a mobile phone. "We can fix anything. And I mean anything."

"Okay."

"Now do you think you can remember all that, or would you like a little reminder? Like a finger, or a toe. Or perhaps something more personal?"

"No. No, I'll do it."

"Good boy"

"But listen. Do something for me." Rory closed his eyes. "Tell her I love her."

There was a sound at the other end like a hippo breaking wind into a mud flat. A cross between a chuckle and a snort of derision.

"You know I might just do that. It might help keep her sweet." The phone went dead.

Rory replaced the receiver gently on the cradle, as though it had died in his hand. He stared unseeing at the instrument for several minutes while a blizzard of questions swirled uncontrollably round his brain. Who was this man? What did he want? Why Rory? What would he have to do? It was obviously related to Tuesday's shipment, but how? And why? If they were hoping to hijack it why wait until it was safely aboard the frigate?

And what was he going to do? He had promised to help them, but could he do that? Could he put Hannah's life above his duty, and above the lives of others who might die if this lunatic got his hands on a consignment of chemical weapons? His mind went to the Tokyo subway system in March 1995.

But then it returned to Hannah. Could he stand by his principles, and wait for the post each day, wondering if there would be part of her in a package?

And on a practical level, if he did go along with them, how could he persuade Terry to swap places with him?

He paced around the flat for nearly an hour, running these questions through his mind, trying to answer them in a way that gave him some control over the situation.

There was one possibility: he could tell Duncan about the phone call. Duncan could substitute Rory for Terry, and be prepared for The Voice to move.

But how much more prepared could they be, than to be on a fully armed warship, with a crew of three hundred? If The Voice thought he could still get away with something, the logical thing for Duncan to do was cancel the trip.

And then what price Hannah's chances?

At last, exhausted through frustration and anger, Rory went to the kitchen and recovered the bottle of single malt his grandfather had given him two Hogmanays ago in a vain attempt to teach him to like the stuff. He broke the seal, poured himself three fingers, and began systematically to take leave of his senses.

. . .

The next morning, Saturday, Rory woke at his usual time with a splitting headache. He lay in till 7.30, then rose, took two paracetamol with a cup of strong coffee, had a cold shower and went for an eight mile run. By 9.30, as he consumed a large plate of scrambled egg on toast, he felt considerably less disembodied. The sense of shock and desperation of the previous night had gone, and although the circumstances had not changed he felt able to consider them with a level head.

He broke the problem down into manageable parts. The first question was whether to confide in Duncan or go along, for the moment at least, with The Voice's demands. Much as he trusted and respected his Chief, Duncan would give no special weight to Hannah's safety. He would, quite properly, consider what was in the interest of National Security, and while Hannah would play a part in his thinking, it would be a small part.

However, if Rory could somehow persuade Terry Davidson to swap places he would have bought time for Hannah without giving anything away. After all, if the coin had come down tails he would have been going anyway. The crunch would come later, presumably when they were on the Lysander, and then, if necessary, he could tell Duncan.

The next problem was how to persuade Terry to swap places, and this was not so easy. He could, of course, ask him as a favour, but he could not think of a single convincing reason to give. And what if he refused? He could try to bribe him, but then Terry would definitely smell a rat, and friend or no friend he should and would report the approach to Duncan.

He could confide in Terry. Tell him about The Voice, but again Rory did not think so little of his colleague as to assume he would lightly let friendship take precedence over duty.

77

Which left the uncomfortable alternative of enforcing the issue. Somehow he would have to make it impossible for Terry to make the trip, in which case Rory would be asked to fill in. But that was considerably less easy than it sounded, and Rory spent the rest of the morning reviewing the possibilities.

He checked the rota to see what shifts were being worked. As seniors, he and Terry worked odd hours in order to overlap with each of the five teams for supervision, and with each other to allow for management meetings with Duncan and Ben Knight. Today Terry was working 08.00 to 16.00, and he was on again Sunday night, 22.00 to 06.00 and Tuesday 20.00 to 04.00.

That meant he would stay on site Monday day time, and sleep in his staff flat. Which immediately limited the possibilities. If he disappeared he would be missed almost immediately. He was also very capable of looking after himself, and would be within the secure confines of Lairig the whole time. It was a tall order.

Suppose he received a message that he was needed at the bedside of a dying relative?

He'd check it out.

Or supposing he got arrested? Rory could plant some cannabis in his flat and anonymously call the police. It would not be difficult. Rory had not done two years in the police force without learning how and where to get hold of the drug. But it could backfire if they accepted Terry's word that it had been planted, and if it did work it would ruin Terry's career. That would be a high price to pay, even to save Hannah

If, on the other hand, Terry was ill...

It was the only way, and it meant Rory making him ill. Poisoning him with something that would put him out of action for twenty-four hours. It was drastic and risky, but then so was the situation.

Rory left for work at 9.30 that evening, still mulling this over in his mind. The thing he most disliked about it was that he would have to rely on The Voice to supply a suitable nostrum. He continued to wrestle with the problem, racking his brain for alternative solutions, throughout what was luckily a quiet shift, but by the time he arrived home at eight o'clock on Sunday morning he had resolved nothing.

78

He showered, slept for four hours, and when he woke still none the wiser reluctantly looked out the phone number he had been given, and rang it.

It was not The Voice who answered, but a quite different, cultured baritone who politely asked him what he wanted.

"My name is Kilbride. I was given this number in case I needed anything."

"Quite so. And how may we help you, Mr. Kilbride?"

"I need to arrange for someone to be out of action for twenty-four hours. I want something that will make him ill, but not seriously so."

"That is not a problem. If you will just give me his name and address."

"No. I will handle it. I just want you to supply the necessary. He is a friend of mine, and apart from anything else he is safe inside a high security establishment, and will not be coming out."

"I see. Well perhaps it would be better if you do it yourself. Though you should not assume that Lairig a' Mhuic is necessarily beyond our sphere of influence."

Rory was taken aback. "What are you saying?"

"I'm saying I shall get you a medicament which will have the effect you require. I take it we are talking about a fit adult?"

"Yes. Male. Thirty-one years old, about twelve stone." So this man was tied in with whoever had hit him over the head, and tried to run him down with the Fordson! "And listen, like I said this is a friend of mine. Whatever you send must be safe, you understand? I shall try it on my cat first, and if it does anything more than honk on the floor all bets are off."

"Very interesting, but for one thing. You do not have a cat, Mr. Kilbride." Once again Rory was caught off guard. Who were these people? "But do not fear. We do not want any unnecessary complications. And I am quite aware that if you were to become convinced that we are unprincipled killers you would have little reason to cooperate with us.

"We do have principles, Rory, even if we have to fight for them. My pledge to you is that if you do what we ask, then Hannah will be returned to you safe and well. If you don't... Well then it is beyond my powers. I am just a cog in a wheel, I'm afraid. Just a cog in a wheel."

Following instructions Rory entered the phone box on the corner of Rosamund Street at 8 pm precisely, and rang the number of the mobile. It was answered by the same man.

"If you look to your right there is a blue car. Do you see it?"

"Yes."

"And beyond that a house with a black door?"

"Yes."

"Count three houses back from there."

Rory counted. "Okay. I have it."

"The house is covered in ivy?"

"Yes."

"And in the front garden are two trees?"

"I see them."

"The smaller of the two is a magnolia, with three main branches."

"Right."

"Your package is in the litter bin at the other end of the street. Good luck."

The phone went dead, leaving Rory fuming that once again he had been so easily wrong-footed. It was so obvious. While he had been foolishly counting houses and trees they had been planting the stuff in full view of the telephone box. They could not risk a tramp turning up looking for sandwiches or cigarette ends, or someone dumping rubbish on top of their parcel, so they had waited till the last moment and then politely asked Rory to look the other way. And he had obediently done so. Some security officer! He walked down the road, cursing roundly at himself.

Sitting on top of the bin, in plain view, was a standard NHS prescription bag. He did not open it till he was home, and inside he found a small dispensing bottle of the type used for ear or eye drops. It was about a third full of a clear liquid, and bore a truncated computer-printed label. Presumably the missing portion had displayed the name of a chemist shop. The label bore the message: 'Mr. R. Kilbride. 3 to 5 drops as necessary. Keep out of the reach of children.'

Rory went on duty at six the next morning with the bottle nestling in his pocket. It was Monday, and he had just this one day in which to act. Terry had worked 22.00 to 06.00, so he was coming off duty as

80

Rory went on. This was not good. The canteen did not open until eight, so Terry would go to his flat, grab some food, and go to bed. There was no convincing way Rory could invite him to breakfast.

If Terry slept for seven hours he would wake around 13.00. The question was whether he would then eat in his flat, or come down to the cafe or restaurant. The odds were about even.

Rory immersed himself in paperwork and passed the morning checking the overtime and sickness returns, and the holiday rotas. At twelve, the earliest he thought Terry might rise, he went over the the water filtration and chlorination plant at the rear of the swimming pool. From here he could see anybody coming down the hill from the residential area. He removed the top from one of the tanks, and took down the long-handled ladle with which samples were taken. If anyone came in he was doing a routine check.

It was a long vigil. Seventy-five minutes might go quickly enough in other circumstances, but standing waiting for something which might not happen, it is a long time. At one fifteen the familiar figure of Terry Davidson finally came loping down the hill towards the recreation block, and Rory closed the tank and hung up the ladle and walked round the rec. so he could meet Terry at the main door.

"Hi Rory. How you doing?"

"Fine. And you?"

"Good. Are you going for lunch?"

"Yes." Rory took this as an invitation, whether it had been intended that way or not. "Cafe or restaurant?"

"Don't mind. Any preference?"

"Yes. I think I fancy the restaurant." It would be emptier, and therefore better for what he had to do.

"Okay." They went up the stairs, and right into the establishment that was known affectionately, if unfairly, as 'The Gristly Rissole'.

So far, Rory thought, it could not have gone more smoothly, but almost as he thought it things began to turn pear-shaped. As they walked in Terry saw Tim Oliver eating with Dr. Goodyear, and went over to them. After a moment's chat he agreed that he and Rory would join them for lunch. Rory swore inwardly, but there was nothing he could do about it. He took his seat politely with the others.

At least he was sitting next to Terry. If Goodyear and Oliver had been sitting opposite each other he would have been across the table from him. Even so, the task was virtually impossible. It was one thing to distract Terry's attention sufficiently to dose his lunch, but to distract three pairs of eyes was something else. And if he was caught with a medicine dropper in his hand....

If his mind had not been wholly preoccupied he would have enjoyed the lunch. Anthony Goodyear was good company. He was younger than the other two Department heads, probably in his early thirties. A large man, with long red hair which he tied back in a ponytail, and a thick beard, he looked more like a heavy-metal disc jockey than a scientist. But then most scientists do not look like scientists.

They talked about politics, jazz and alternative medicine, and Goodyear was well informed on all of them. He treated each with disrespectful good humour, frequently causing laughter among his companions.

But Rory did not take it in. He tried to stop himself watching Terry's every mouthful, as the food on his plate slowly disappeared. With an increasing sense of urgency he saw the main course cleared away and the desserts arrive. He hoped beyond hope that Goodyear and Oliver would leave when they finished, but instead they lingered on, debating whether acupuncture was quackery or ancient wisdom. They were still there when Rory and Terry ordered coffee, and they were still there when it was drunk and the bills were presented.

He had failed. He bade them all a friendly farewell, but his smile faded as soon as his back was turned, and there was an annoyed scowl of concentration on his face as he walked slowly back to his office.

What now?

He was off duty in five minutes time. No-one would would be surprised if he stayed around, which was something, but while he and Terry were colleagues with a good social relationship, they were not so close that he could hang around on street corners waiting to eat every meal with him. Their lunch today was probably the first such shared meal for a month, and to repeat it in the evening would be distinctly strange.

The only alternative was to get into Terry's flat, and dose his food, but Terry had gone back there, so it was out of the question till he went back on duty at 8.00 pm. Rory spent the afternoon in the gym and sauna, and had a leisurely supper in the canteen. Tantalisingly Terry came in with a couple of others, and sat two tables away. Once again Rory had to force himself not to watch each forkful making its way to his mouth.

At 8.15 Rory saw Terry taking two new recruits on the back of a tractor down towards the stores and workshop, and seized his chance. He walked up the main path - very few people would question his presence there at that time, and nothing would look more suspicious than skulking through the trees - and turned right. The flats provided for single auxiliaries were in a group on their own, less scenically sited then the scientists' houses.

Terry's door was unlocked - people rarely locked doors at Lairig - and Rory let himself in and shut it behind him, as certain as he could be that he was unobserved.

He went straight to the kitchen and looked round. It was neat and tidy, the surfaces clear with no food in site. He opened each cupboard in turn, and found in the front of one an opened box of breakfast cereal. He then found the fridge, and inside the door an opened bottle of milk. He took the top off the bottle and sniffed - no point dosing a bottle of sour milk which would be thrown away. But it smelt fine. He took the medicine bottle from his pocket, gave it a precautionary shake, unscrewed the top and squeezed the rubber bulb to charge the glass stem of the dropper. With the pipette poised over the the milk bottle he debated with himself how much to put in. The dose was three to five drops, but would Terry drink the whole bottle? Suppose he just had a cup of tea. He wouldn't use a tenth of the milk. On the other hand, if Rory was too generous, and Terry came home thirsty and swigged the lot, it might do more than just upset his stomach.

Rory carefully counted eight drops, and replaced the stopped. He put the flat of his hand over the neck of the milk bottle, and shook it thoroughly. He replaced the foil top, put it back in the fridge, and washed his hands.

There were any number of ifs - what if Terry had a cooked breakfast? Or heated the milk - would the stuff still work? Or what if he drank too much, or too little, or had breakfast in the canteen?

Rory shrugged mentally as he left the flat. He had done what he could; it was now in the lap of the gods. He was logged out of the gates of Lairig a' Mhuic at 8.35 pm and was in bed by ten thirty.

His last thoughts before he fell asleep were of Hannah.

. . .

Howsafe Ltd. was an expanding concern. It had recently moved into the area of industrial security, offering among other things an anti-espionage service. It was quite natural, therefore, that in the offices above a hardware store in Finsbury Park there were, lying around, various devices for detecting illicit bugs. Ostensibly they were there to demonstrate to prospective clients, but from time to time they had their other uses. Richard Warrender had completed a thorough sweep of their own premises earlier that morning.

Toshihiko arrived first. He greeted Warrender and accepted a drink, which he took over to the window where he could watch the comings and goings of the human zoo below.

It was not long before he saw Gordon Carpenter's car pull into the last space in the small office car park, and its owner climb out. Watching him walk towards the building he thought what an intelligent touch the moustache and watch chain were. Gordon had a hard face. Cruel almost. But the oversized moustache disguised this well, adding a slightly humorous touch, and the watch chain distracted the eye and suggested, in one so young, a degree of affectation and fogeyism which again wholly belied the truth about the man who wore it.

Gordon had every reason to look hard. If the face is the nearest thing to a window into the soul, the view through this one was hardly bathed in the light of human kindness. His father, a cold and inaccessible man, taught the classics at a public school. His mother, a dutiful and caring woman, tried her best for her children, but her own life was a constant struggle against the demons of schizophrenia, and when Gordon was six she lost that battle and took her own life.

His father's reaction, or rather lack of reaction, was typical of the man. Incapable of mourning or expressing his grief, he refused to speak about her death or reminisce about her life. At the same time he became even more remote and offhand in his dealings with those around him; not least his sons. The youngest of these, Gordon, continued an increasingly unhappy existence at his father's school, forced to internalise and repress his own sense of loss and anger and injustice.

Distanced from his peers because his father was a none too popular teacher, and distanced from his father by his inability to show his son any form of affection, his years at school were solitary and bleak. When the time came to leave he finally defied his father for the first time in any real way by enrolling at London University to study psychology instead of the approved course of a red-brick university to read classics. But it was a Pyrrhic victory, because by now his father's indifference was almost absolute.

His choice of subject may have been influenced, however unconsciously, by a desire to annoy his father and at the same time try to reach some understanding of his own psychopathology. His experiences at university were infinitely happier than they were at school, especially after he met Richard Warrender and Toshihiko Yamamoto. Like many unhappy children he had found solace in the world of trees and animals, and with their influence quickly developed into a single-minded environmental activist.

He was by nature, perhaps, not quite as casually ruthless as they were: in the early days he had worried about the possibility that one of their bombs might injure or kill someone, while they took the line that there were always casualties in war, and if it happened, so be it.

He had come a long way since then!

From his vantage point at the window above, Yamamoto watched his young colleague walk towards the building. Tosh did not much care for psychology himself, but he still could not help wondering. What were the odds against the three of them all losing their mothers in their early childhood? And then going on to form this triumvirate - for what? Gaia. The Earth Goddess. Mother Nature.

What would the monstrous regiment of head-shrinkers and socio-psychobabblers make of that? He shuddered at the thought that they might one day get the opportunity.

When Gordon entered the room, Richard served him a fruit juice and sat him down, and Toshihiko went straight into his presentation.

He began by detailing the security arrangements being made for the transport of the T2, and having dismissed the possibility of lifting it either from Lairig a' Mhuic or en route to Aberdeen, he outlined a breathtakingly audacious plan to spirit it away from the frigate in mid ocean. At first the idea struck Richard as ludicrous, but as Tosh went on, slowly explaining in his impeccable English both the practicalities and psychology of his idea, the more Richard came to believe it might work.

When Tosh finished Richard gave an account of his own findings. He had identified three safe houses in different parts of the world which they could use once they had the chemical. He had arranged complex channels of communication for negotiation with the Authorities, through which they could not be traced. He had laboratory facilities lined up for diluting the T2 and repackaging it as required. He had drawn up provisional outline plans for a number of small demonstrations, and he had a private plane and a well equipped yacht standing by. These were both owned by a playboy millionaire and long-time supporter, who was apparently unaware of the irony of someone of his extravagant lifestyle backing a movement such as theirs. This irony did not trouble Richard. He was happy to use the man, as he would use any resource, just as he would happily see him damned with all the others when the time of reckoning arrived.

When Richard finished it was Gordon's turn, and there was a short hiatus while he prepared. He opened his briefcase, and from it took a laptop computer and a box containing about thirty-five floppy disks. These were partitioned off in several sections labelled with business applications, and one, at the back of the box, labelled 'Games'. Gordon took out one of these called 'Chevron Blaster' and loaded it into his computer. The game was genuine and playable, but Gordon was interested only in the package of binary digits hidden within the machine code on the disk. He downloaded this into his laptop and refiled the disk.

He then selected another disk from the box entitled 'Sales Figures: Sept. '94 - May '95'. Booted up in the normal way this too would appear innocuous, but once again what Gordon wanted was a small programme buried beneath one of the files, invisible to all but the most keen eyed computer expert.

Again he downloaded, typed in a seventeen word sentence, and then brief instructions which told the programme from the sales disk to decode the information from the games disk using the letters of the sentence as the key. In a few seconds the screen was filled with plain script, to which he referred as he addressed the others

"Our first problem is that no-one outside Lairig a' Mhuic knows about the T2, or what it can do. Or at least no-one does officially. As soon as we acquire it, therefore, we will need to share the glad tidings with the world. We shall contact Sir Graham Huish in the first instance, and inform him that he either persuades the media of the power of the stuff, or we arrange a demonstration. Once he tells them what effect a few milligrams aerosolled into a major subway system would have, the world's press will go ape. You can imagine the headlines for yourself.

"I then suggest we give them a week or so to sweat. This will feed their fear and paranoia, and get them nice and ripe for the next phase.

"Which is issuing our demands. My first thought was to compile a list and a timetable by which they were to be met. However this has a number of snags, not least of which is verification. The things we really want to achieve - an end to all deforestation, boreal and tropical, for example - are impossible to monitor. How are we to know what is happening in Siberia and Alaska and Amazonia? And what would we do about non-compliance? We would run a serious risk of making ourselves look foolish.

"The only way to achieve our wider goal is to win people over and change attitudes, and I believe we can do this. We start by making one major demand to establish our credentials and get the ball rolling. I propose this should be the immediate halting of all private car manufacture in Europe, North America and Japan.

"Now of course that is going to hurt, and the resistance will be phenomenal. With the knock-on effect in other trades we are talking about tens of thousands out of work. The response will undoubtedly be the standard line that you cannot afford to give in to terrorism, and that business will continue as usual, even though we shall make it clear that our first demonstrations will be in offending communities."

"At which point we can assume our bluff will be called." Gordon paused, and looked at his colleagues. "And I am afraid, we shall have to arrange a demonstration. I honestly don't believe we will get any concessions otherwise, regrettable as it may be.

"Are we all okay on this?" he asked, knowing what the answer would be.

"I am," Tosh nodded.

"Yes," Richard agreed easily.

"Right." Gordon continued, amused at how calmly he himself now considered the prospect of mass murder. "So we show then what we can do. Meanwhile Professor Huish will be telling them that we have enough of the chemical to go on giving similar demonstrations almost indefinitely. They are forced to close the factories, and car production halts in the developed world. This will cause all sorts of excitement, and we shall need to give them time to get used to it. We shall suggest that they can avoid total economic chaos by redirecting private car capacity into public transport - turn the production lines over to buses, trams and trains.

"At the same time we demand a complete revamping of the tax structure along the lines of the polluter pays, and the reconvenning of the UN Conference on Environment and Development - the so-called Earth Summit. Only this time we write the agenda; an International agenda addressing the issues not just of ecological destruction in the Third World, but over consumption and energy use in Western countries.

"And we shall set minimum targets to be met. Instead of the farce we had in Rio in 1993 we shall expect serious action on a global scale. This will gain us a lot of support. There are large numbers of people - not least AOSIS, the Alliance of Small Island States - who were pig-sick at the lack of commitment before and would be delighted to see the Conference reconvened with the balance tilted towards the environment instead of big business and the political interests of the minority of industrialised nations.

"And even though they'll bellyache about making policy with a gun to their heads, once they start making commitments to change they will be held to them.

"And I envisage that in time we shall see opinion moving over to our side as people come to appreciate what we are doing, and we shall come to be seen not as terrorists, but as the people who saved the

Earth."

Gordon closed the top of his laptop, and finished his fruit juice.

"Thank you for that, Gordon," Richard told him. "A very comprehensive piece of work." Toshihiko added his approval.

Gordon was delighted by this unusual display of approbation.

Fifteen minutes later, after Gordon had left, Toshihiko stood watching the street below. Richard sat at the table, thoughtfully turning a pencil in his hands.

"Do you think we've covered everything?"

There was a long pause. So long that someone who did not know Tosh, and his capacity for thinking before he spoke, might have thought he had not heard. When he did speak he did not turn away from the window. "I don't think we've even touched first base," he said evenly. "And nor do you." Only then did he turn towards his companion, and for a long moment the two men held each other's eyes, wordlessly feeling their way into forbidden territory. "Go on," Richard coaxed him, his voice and his face expressionless.

Toshihiko turned back to the window and watched a large, red, double-decker bus disgorging its cargo of shoppers and commuters onto the pavement.

"The problem is not whether people drive cars or travel by bus. Nor is a reconvened Earth Summit going to make any real impression. If we're going to leave it to politicians to solve, even with our gun at their heads, then we might as well give up now.

"The problem, as we both know, is the people themselves. Even if they were rational, and prepared to live a simple life in harmony with nature, there would still be too many of them. Six billion, and rising by quarter of a million a day. The planet simply cannot support them.

"And they are not rational, and never will be. Those who have televisions and foreign holidays and electric hair-curlers want more and better, and those who haven't got them want them. Any leader or government who tried to take these toys away wouldn't last five minutes. They would simply get rid of them and find someone else who would let them carry on blindly murdering the planet and digging their grand-children's graves - if not their children's.

"And even if we manage to bully them into making a few reforms,

89

that isn't going to solve anything. We can't hold a gun to the world's head indefinitely. The only long term solutions require good will, self-sacrifice, organisation, consensus of opinion, and trust." He turned to face Richard. "Do you see those things in abundance among your fellow beings? Because I don't.

"How many civil wars are there going on at this very moment? If people can't get along and agree with their next door neighbours to save their own lives, what hope is there of persuading them to give up their comforts and conveniences and luxuries because of some abstract notion about the health of the planet?"

Richard stood up and walked over to stand shoulder to shoulder with him. "So what are you saying?" he asked very quietly.

"I'm saying what you're thinking. I'm saying there is only one solution, and that it is in our hands."

"Could you do it?"

"I don't know. I honestly don't know." He quietly contemplated what he was proposing. "It's not dying that bothers me, it's the other lives. So many other lives. I wonder. If your cause is just, is it worse to kill a million people - or a billion - than to kill one?

"And do the deaths really matter in the end? After all we would only be hastening the inevitable. But still...." His mind seemed reluctant to contemplate the enormity of it.

"What do you think would happen?"

"If we released it? With no demands and no warning? High altitude fine aerosol dispersal across the globe? From what I can gather we would almost certainly eliminate between thirty and fifty per cent of the human race, possibly double that."

"Sixty per cent would stop the destruction in its tracks. Even forty and it would probably never recover. Industry is too complex, too interdependent to survive. The people who remained would be forced to adopt a simple lifestyle."

"It wouldn't take them that long to rebuild. The knowledge would still be there."

"I'm not so sure. They'd have to repopulate first, and that would take generations. Many generations - bear in mind the death rate would get back to normal, with no immunisation programmes, no hospitals and high-tech health care artificially making sick people well, and old people live longer. And during this time the knowledge and skill base would be dwindling."

"And all the time the planet would be repairing herself. The rain forests could regenerate, the ozone layer would heal, the oceans would slowly detoxify themselves... It would mean Gaia could survive."

"Yes." Tosh looked intense, excited.

Richard stared out of the window. "What do you reckon would be the effect on the rest of the animal kingdom?

"Well nerve agents work on the central nervous system, so it could effect all mammals. We'd certainly lose a lot of charismatic megafauna to mass extinctions. But if things go on as they are they will all be extinct soon anyway. And ninety-nine point nine per cent of living things would survive: the insects, nematodes, arthropods, protozoa. And of course the viruses and bacteria. The things on which Gaia depends, the things which really matter."

Richard looked at him and nodded slowly. "But could you do it?" he asked again.

Toshihiko held his eyes for a long moment. "Yes," he said finally. "I could do it."

Richard threw his arms round him and hugged him. "You know, Tosh, I love you like a brother."

"I know." Toshihiko looked at the younger man with a mixture of affection and regret. "It is good that we should die together. I wonder what sort of death it will be? Fairly quick, but very unpleasant, I should imagine. We must stay close to each other. We should be together at the end."

"You take the prospect of death very calmly," Richard said warmly.

The shadow of the smile still played at the corners of Tosh's mouth. "It is expected. It is a tradition of my Country."

"Horsefeathers. Don't give me that kamikaze crap," Richard said, deliberately lightening the mood. "But supposing I said we didn't have to die. What would you say?"

"I would say that we are not immortal, Richard. And there is no antidote to this substance. If it blows round the world at random, there will be nowhere that is safe."

Richard grinned. "You are wrong, though. There is a place. One

91

place that has its own atmosphere, that grows its own food, sealed off from the rest of world. A place that has its own ocean..."

"Its own desert, rainforest, farm..." Tosh almost shouted, striking his forehead with his palm. "Son of a gun! I've been so wrapped up in all this I'd completely forgotten it. Of course! Biosphere II. But that's brilliant. When did you... You didn't..." He thought for a moment. "No, of course not. You wouldn't have known about the T2 then."

"No. It was pure luck. Or perhaps it was more than that. It's hard to believe it wasn't meant to happen. Perhaps Gaia arranged it," he said, half seriously.

Tosh nodded. It was a couple of years ago that The Battalions had put in a bid for the lease of Biosphere II, the hermetically sealed geodesic glass dome built in the Arizona desert by a Texas millionaire. The three and a half acre site, containing 3,800 species of animal, an artificial ocean with forty-two species of fish and thirty-five of coral, and a farm which produces three crops a year, form a totally self-sufficient 'Earth within the Earth'.

Once the original experiment came to a rather abrupt end, the management team were sacked, and the centre was put on a business footing, it was inevitable that The Battalions would want a piece of the action. It could have been designed for them: indeed, if it had not already existed they might well have come up with something similar. As it was they had made a preliminary bid for a three year tenure, which had been accepted and signed up twelve months previously. They had nicknamed the project "Daughter of Gaia."

The original plan had been for the legitimate wing of the organisation to carry out a programme of scientific research, which they would combine with a high profile publicity campaign and recruitment drive. The team to be sealed in the $150 million building had already been picked, and were due to begin their experiment in a couple of months, but it would be no problem to make a few changes, and include certain hand picked individuals who would bind the crew into a tightknit team of specialists, ready to come out when the time was ripe, and teach what was left of the human race to live a sustainable life in harmony with Gaia.

Toshihiko shook his head in admiration at his erstwhile pupil. It was brilliant. Simply brilliant.

92

CHAPTER 5

On Tuesday morning Rory woke at his usual time and two thoughts, which had not been there the previous evening, monopolised his mind. He had been so wound up in his concern for Hannah that he had given no consideration to the broader view, but as so often happens the subconscious mind had been turning matters over, and now, on waking, presented its findings. And they were not comforting. Rory climbed under the shower and considered the situation.

The only thing The Voice had asked him do was to be aboard the *Lysander*, and do what he was told. Which meant there had to be someone else aboard to do the telling. And that person, he suddenly realised with startling clarity, had to be Dr. Anthony Goodyear. He could eliminate the ship's crew, and that left only himself, Duncan and Dr. Goodyear. And unbelievable though it seemed, it did make sense. The Voice had inside knowledge. No-one outside Lairig was supposed to know about the shipment leaving later in the day, and yet the man on the phone knew more than Rory did. It was he who had told him the name of the *Lysander*.

He could only have learned that from someone high up in Lairig. And that someone, who was also the shadowy figure whom Rory had chased round the campus in the middle of the night with such painful consequences, could be none other than Dr. Goodyear.

And that made the second thought all the more unsavoury. Supposing the deaths of Skinner and Dobbs had something to do with this? It was, after all, immediately after they died that things began to happen at Lairig.

And if they were related the question arose: did they really commit suicide, or could it have been murder? Could Goodyear have killed them?

As soon as Rory got to work he would check whether Goodyear had left the base that night.

It also meant that Goodyear was connected with, if not personally involved in, Hannah's abduction. Beneath the flow of hot water Rory shivered

93

But at least he now knew the face of the enemy, and one thing was certain, whatever else happened, once Hannah was safe he would make Dr. Anthony Goodyear pay very dearly for his part in this.

Rory arrived for work early as usual. He was anxious to find out if there was any news of Terry, but first he went to Duncan's office. The Chief was not there, but his secretary let Rory in, and waited unquestioningly while he checked the Entries and Exits Register in which the staff on the gate log everybody in and out of Lairig. On the night Skinner and Dobbs died Dr. Goodyear had not left the complex.

So he had not done the dirty work in person: not that that improved his standing in Rory's eyes one bit.

Rory went to the Canteen for breakfast. He was ravenous, and if all went according to plan this would be a long day. He helped himself to bacon, sausage, egg, mushroom, tomatoes and fried bread, and a cup of tea, and chose an empty table as he did not feel like socialising. He sat with his food and his crossword, but did not concentrate on either. His thoughts were elsewhere.

Terry should have finished work a couple of hours ago. Hopefully he then went home and at least made himself a cup of tea. How long would the concoction take to work? Minutes? Hours? If he had been taken ill straight away he would have phoned for the M.O., and Rory, as Senior on call, would have heard.

Rory picked up a piece of sausage on his fork, and lifted it to his mouth. But it did not quite make it to its destination. The hand that was raising it froze as Terry Davidson walked into the room.

His hair was all over the place and there was sweat breaking out on his face. He looked awful, and Rory felt a mixture of guilt and relief, though both emotions faded rapidly when Terry went to the counter and ordered a breakfast almost as big as Rory's. He had not come in search of assistance, but of food.

Terry hefted his tray, saw Rory sitting alone, and perhaps because of his hospitality the previous day, went over to his table.

"Mind if I join you?"

"No, of course not."

"I should be in bed by rights. I was off at six, but could I sleep? I gave up after an hour and I've been playing squash with Joe. I'm hoping the exercise and some cholesterol will help me get off. It's a bummer, because I've got this trip tonight. Funny how you can never sleep when you really need to."

Rory, who had never had that problem, sympathised.

Terry finished emptying his tray onto the table, returned it to the nearest rack, and then excused himself to go to the lavatory. Rory sat staring at the plate of food opposite him. He was alone with Terry's breakfast. No one was watching. He had all the time in the world.

And the medicine bottle was in his car.

It had never occurred to him that Terry would turn up for breakfast, two hours after the end of a night shift. He had no reason to, but that did not stop him burning with a sense of anger and self-reproach.

Terry returned and chatted through the meal, and eventually went back to his flat to try once more to sleep.

Rory went to work.

He was by nature an easy-going man, who took most things in his stride. He was certainly not much given to panic, but he was close to it this day. With Terry fit and well he had no fall-back plan, and he could not get out of his head images of Skinner and Dobbs, and how they might have met their deaths. And of Hannah.

He did very little work that day, and spent most of his time staying out of the way of other people. At 4.00 pm he reached a conclusion. He either had to put on a balaclava and go to Terry's flat and lay about him with a blunt instrument, or confess all to Duncan.

As he entered the office Duncan was in the act of replacing the handset on the telephone. He raised an eyebrow at Rory's appearance.

"I need to speak to you, Duncan. It's important."

At that point the pager on Rory's belt began to bleep, and he looked down to read the message.

"It's all right," Duncan told him. "It's me. I was just getting the switchboard call you. It's also important, but let's hear what you wanted first."

On an intuition Rory said: "No, that's all right. It's important, but it's not urgent. And you called me first."

"Okay. I've just been informed that Terry Davidson has gone down with gastroenteritis. I know it's short notice, but could you stand in for him on the trip to Johnston?" Rory's chest felt as though a rhinoceros had stepped off it. "I need someone I can rely on, and I wouldn't ask you at this late hour if it wasn't important," Duncan went on unnecessarily.

Rory appeared to consider the problem for a moment, not wanting to appear too keen. "No problem," he said at last. "There's nothing I can't cancel."

"Good man. We leave here around eight." Duncan looked at his watch. "That gives you four hours, although you could add a bit if needs be. Is that enough time to get home and pack and make the necessary arrangements?"

"Just about."

"Better get to it then." Duncan smiled his thanks and valediction. "Oh, by the way. What was it you wanted?"

Rory turned, half way to the door. "I'll tell you when I get back. There'll be more time then."

"Fair enough."

Outside, he could barely contain his relief. The sense of reprieve was almost tangible. Whatever the trip ahead held he had done what The Voice demanded. There was no need yet for Hannah to be hurt.

Four and a quarter hours later Rory once more pulled up outside the Administration block. In the car park were four large, dark, anonymous family saloons which he did not recognise. He went through the main entrance, and found the vestibule full of people.

There were at least a dozen men standing around, four of them uniformed and armed policemen, the rest almost certainly their plain-clothes colleagues; large, quiet, competent looking men with watchful eyes. Rory walked through them to his Chief's office where he found further visitors: a senior police officer, Dr. Goodyear, and Drs Roper and Wilson. Rory looked at them in undisguised surprise.

"Ah, Rory, come in." Duncan waved him to an empty chair. "Let me put you in the picture.

"I may have led you to believe that Dr. Roper and Dr. Wilson were not involved in this trip. In fact they are coming with us. The material we are taking is in a TCR," he indicated the four on his desk, "and it is particularly unstable and unpleasant. Because of that I want the best brains on hand in case of problems."

"Is this a last minute decision, or was it planned all along?"

"All along. But if we had said a week ago that all three were sailing to Johnston it would have caused talk and suspicion. And I have been keeping security as tight as possible. It's nothing personal. Terry didn't know either."

Rory swallowed hard. It was not his pride that was damaged, but now he no longer knew who the enemy was. He looked at each of the scientists in turn. It could be any one of them. The only crumb of comfort he had in this whole wretched business was gone.

"It's a bit extreme, isn't it?"

"Possibly, but this is not like shipping defunct warheads or missiles. If anyone got their hands on this they could take it away on a bicycle. And I have reason to believe someone is already interested in it."

"In stealing it?"

"Possibly, yes."

Presumably the prowler, Rory thought. But he had been forbidden to mention him, and unsure whether that prohibition still stood in these new circumstances, he said: "Do you know who?"

"No. I've no idea."

Was that true, Rory wondered, or did he not want to talk in front of the others? He would have to find out more, but this was not the time or the place.

"As I say," Duncan continued, "one of these TCRs contains the agent, the others are decoys. One has already left, and the next one can go any minute. That was to be Terry's, though I could put you to the end if you still have things to do."

"No. I'm ready when you are."

"In that case," Duncan said rising, "I'll see you to your car." He handed Rory a TCR and walked out to the vestibule where a driver and two escorts were assigned to the trip.

"See you in Aberdeen," Duncan called, as they left the building.

. . .

Captain North dropped the paper he was reading face down on the coffee table beside his chair, and called "Come". Petty Officer Ordish entered, his cap under his arm.

"The first man from Lairig a' Mhuic has arrived, sir."

North grunted. "Show him to his quarters and then stick him in the wardroom with a drink. And do the same with the others when they turn up."

"Very good sir." The man turned and left, the trace of a grin forming on his face as soon as the curtain of the Commanding Officer's day cabin had closed behind him. He's not pleased, he thought to himself. Not pleased at all.

When he was alone North crossed to the porthole, and looked down at the midnight blue Rover standing on the concrete apron below him. The three men who had climbed out had been joined by two of the ship's gangway staff, and were standing in a group. One of them wore the uniform of a police marksman, complete with body armour, and cradled a Heckler and Koch machine gun in his arms. North returned to his work.

On the quay the group opened up as P.O. Ordish approached them. "I believe one of you gentlemen is sailing with us?"

"Yes." Anthony Goodyear identified himself.

"Very good, sir. If you would care to come with me." He turned to the two sailors. "Bring Dr. Goodyear's luggage to his cabin." While the men lifted the bags out of the boot Goodyear leant into the car and picked up the TCR from the back seat.

"The men will carry that for you, sir." Ordish offered.

"Thanks, but I'd as soon hang onto it."

"As you wish, sir. I take it that's what all the fuss is about?"

Goodyear glanced at the steel cylinder in his hands. "It could be, but then again it could be full of tap water for all I know." As they walked up the gangway he explained the system of decoys.

Must be something very nasty," Ordish observed. "We've got eighty warheads full of Sarin, and thirty-five of cyanogen chloride on board already, and they didn't have decoys."

"It is pretty nasty," Goodyear conceded, thinking as he did so, that that had to be the understatement of the decade. "It was an experimental number which turned out to be particularly unpredictable."

"Right, well when we know which is the real one we will put it somewhere good and safe. Now this is your cabin, sir," Ordish told him, opening a door on his right. "If you would like to stow your gear, seaman Greenhalgh will wait and show you round." He turned to one of the two luggage bearers. "When Dr. Goodyear is ready give him a brief tour of the ship, then take him to the wardroom and get him a drink."

Ordish left them and returned to the gangway, where he instructed the crew to contact him when the next car arrived.

"Not much of a reception the Owner's laid on for them, is it sir?"

Ordish grinned. "You may not have noticed, but there are two things Captain North dislikes intently: freight, and civilian passengers. In his own words he does not run 'a pleasure cruiser or a tramp steamer'."

It was thirty minutes before the ship's main broadcast summoned Ordish back to the gangway, and this time he had two cars to meet.

Although they had left Lairig at different times they had also travelled different routes, and Charlie Wilson's car arrived only a couple of minutes after Rory's. As soon as the Ford Granada pulled to a halt Rory climbed out, grateful to stretch his legs. He looked up at the big warship which was to be his home for the next three weeks: a home to be shared with the man who was party to the murder of Skinner and Dobbs, and the kidnapping of Hannah.

Was it Goodyear, Roper or Wilson? He knew them all, and liked them. It was unthinkable that one of them could be capable of such things, and yet the logic was inescapable. He had thought about nothing else for the last eight hours, and there were still no alternatives.

While he was standing there nursing these dark thoughts M.M's car arrived and its occupants disembarked. While his escorts chatted to the crew of the *Lysander*, Charlie Wilson wandered over to where Rory was standing, and took up a position at his left shoulder. He leaned slightly towards him, and just loud enough to be heard above the throbbing of the ship's auxiliary engines, said: "Never send to know for whom the bell tolls, me old mate. It tolls for thee."

Rory spun round, his mouth half open, his eyes wider than normal. "You!" he exploded in an involuntary burst of venom and disbelief. Of the three he had prayed it would not be M.M.

Wilson was clearly taken aback by this response, but his tone was even as he responded. "No, 'thee'. It's the answer to the crossword, innit? 'Thee' - for whom the bell tolls - it tolls for 'thee'. I got it on the way here."

Rory's shoulders dropped as he emptied his lungs. "I'm sorry, I was miles away. It fit's the letters I suppose?" he tried to gloss over his outburst.

"Oh yeah, it fits." Wilson raised an eyebrow. "I didn't think you were coming. I was told Terry Davidson was joining us."

"He was taken ill at the last minute. I was asked to fill in."

"I see. And you feel all right? You looked as though you'd seen the ghost of 'amlet's father just now."

"No, I'm fine thanks. Just daydreaming." he turned briskly back towards the cars. "Better get those canisters onto the ship and find out where we're sleeping."

Wilson followed him, frowning slightly.

· · ·

Duncan was the last to arrive in the wardroom and add his TCR to the four already on the table. He was greeted by the First Lieutenant, Commander Ussher, who had come to welcome them aboard. Duncan thanked him for his hospitality; a formality since he knew that it had been cleared by the Secretary of State for Defence, and was thus out of Ussher's hands, or those of the Captain for that matter. Duncan accepted the offer of a coffee, and then, taking out his pocket phone, and explaining the procedure to Ussher, phoned Lairig.

His conversation with Graham Huish was brief. He informed him that they had all arrived safely, and learnt from him what he needed to know.

"Right," he said, stowing the phone back in his pocket. "I put the TR2 in number three, and Sir Graham changed three to four, so this," he picked up the canister which Anthony Goodyear had brought, "is the one."

"I take it you would like that stowed somewhere safe?" Ussher offered, and without waiting for a reply went to a microphone on the wall. "First Lieutenant calling, Sergeant of Marines to the wardroom please." Returning to Duncan he said: "We'll lock it up in the armoury. Should be safe enough in there. And these others?" he pointed to the other four. What would you like done with those?"

"It doesn't matter, as long as I have them back. They cost about a hundred and sixty pounds apiece."

Ussher turned to seaman Greenhalgh. "Take those down to the paint store, Roger."

"Yes sir." The young sailor took the first one and left.

While he was gone another man appeared in the room.

"Sir?"

"This is Sgt. Russell," Ussher told Duncan, "our Sergeant of Marines." he turned to the sailor. "I want this cylinder locked in the armoury for the duration of the voyage. No-one is to touch it without Mr. Mclennan's permission."

"Aye aye sir."

"Perhaps you would like to go with Sgt. Russell and see it stowed?" Ussher suggested, and Duncan, grateful for a chance to walk around after the confinement of the car journey, readily accepted the invitation.

By midnight the ship was being closed up ready for sea, and having nothing better to do the civilian passengers were standing on the flight deck taking in the sights and sounds of their surroundings, and watching the activities of the crew as they brought the ship to readiness. The twin Tyne gas turbines that were about to take them halfway round the world were throbbing powerfully beneath their feet, and Rory could almost feel the ship straining at her hawsers in a bid to make for the open sea and freedom.

But what was freedom for the *Lysander* was quite the opposite for him. He would be incarcerated for the next three weeks with three men, one of whom held Hannah's life in his hands.

But at least he had Duncan. Soon he could confide in him. Not at once, because they could still abandon the trip. Have the ship turn back or re-route it. But as soon as they were past the point of no return he could make his confession.

Unless, of course, things began to happen before that.

It was 00.13 when a car drew up alongside the ship, and Petty Officer Ordish appeared on the gangway to meet it. A tall, distinguished-looking man in civilian clothes, one of the Senior Officers Rory guessed, climbed out of the back and was escorted aboard. Almost immediately afterwards the gangway was raised.

Twelve minutes later the *Lysander* eased gently out of her berth, and made her way slowly through the docks towards the sea. Once they had crossed the bar the Tynes began to pick up speed, the twin screws thrusting the ship forward, while thrashing a boiling white wake of aerated brine out behind.

The small group from Lairig remained, watching the lights of Aberdeen slip steadily away. Shortly after 01.00, when Stonehaven was visible on the starboard side, Petty Officer Rose, the Captain's Steward, appeared through the hangar with a tin tray bearing mugs of steaming hot chocolate.

Rory accepted his drink with thanks. "Who was the late arrival?" he asked, raising his voice above the roar of the propellers.

"'Fraid I don't know, sir."

"It wasn't one of the Officers then?"

"No sir. I've never seen the gentleman before."

"And you're not told who is sailing on the ship?"

"Well the Captain told us to expect the five of you, sir. But he didn't mention that other gentlemen. At least not to me."

"Is it usual to have civilian passengers?"

"No sir. Most unusual."

"Thanks." Rory sipped his chocolate thoughtfully. Did this have any significance for him? Could the man be an accomplice? An intermediary? The Voice even?

It was difficult to see how he could have wangled his way on board, but then an organisation that could penetrate the higher echelons of Lairig a' Mhuic was presumably capable of almost anything.

Rory would have to check this man out.

The following morning Rory breakfasted with the three scientists in the officers' mess. Duncan did not appear, and nor did the late arrival of the previous evening.

When he had eaten Rory went to Duncan's cabin. Things had been so hectic in the last twenty-four hours he had not had a chance to talk to him about his suspicions concerning the deaths of Skinner and Dobbs. But he found Duncan suffering from advanced sea-sickness.

"Sorry about this," his Chief whispered through clenched teeth, looking very much as though he meant it. "Bad sailor. Always have been. It's one of the reasons I wanted you along - you'll have to hold the fort for a few days."

"Doing what?" Rory enquired good-humouredly. "Guarding the boffins? Watching out for intruders?"

Duncan attempted to return the grin, but failed spectacularly. The effort brought on a bout of dry retching, which left him exhausted. Eventually he collapsed back onto his pillow, his eyes closed, his face the colour of phlegm.

"I'll see if they have a medic on the ship," Rory offered.

"Don't bother," Duncan said, without opening his eyes. "There's nothing to be done but sit it out. I'll be fine."

Rory left him then, and after a brief walk around the decks returned to his own cabin where he read a book till lunch time.

When he went down to the mess he found the others already there. Roper and M.M. were sitting opposite Goodyear and one of the ship's officers, whom M.M. was entertaining with a favourite conjuring trick. He rolled a green paper serviette into a ball, placed it in his fist, shook it quickly three times, blew on it, and then opened his hand to show it was empty. It was evident he had repeated the trick a number of times from the collection of green paper balls on the floor under his chair.

Rory took the empty chair on Wilson's right, and as he pulled himself in he dropped his fork on the floor. He bent down to retrieve it, and simultaneously pocketed the paper balls. He liked the trick too, though he had learned its simple secret a long time ago, and saw no reason not to help the illusion along a bit.

"Ah, Rory. This is MEO Henry Rankin," M.M. introduced his audience. "MEO stands for Marine Engineer Officer. He keeps the engines going - tweaks the carburettor and changes the spark plugs. That sort of thing."

Rory leaned across the table and shook hands.

"Can you tell me how he makes those napkins disappear?" Rankin asked.

Rory creased his brow. "Well he told me once that he carries round this magic dust that he was given by a pixie, but he's never shown it to me."

Rankin grinned, then lifted the table cloth, bent over, and inspected the floor under Wilson's chair. "It's very good. I shall have to tell Don Crouch, our Entertainments Officer. We shall have you in the next show."

"What show is that?" Roper asked.

"Well things can get pretty boring when you're at sea for any length of time, and it's one of the ways of breaking the monotony. Those who like that sort of thing learn sketches and poems and the like, and some of them can sing, and they put on a show for the rest of the crew. I have to say that when you've seen half a dozen, mostly with all the same cast, they get to be a bit repetitive. But it makes a change from videos."

"If they do one while we're on board I'd be pleased to take part," Wilson agreed. "And Dr. Goodyear here plays a mean saxophone."

"I'll mention it to Don. I don't know what his plans are."

The mystery man of the eleventh hour arrival was also at lunch, but he sat on the opposite side of the room. Rory learned that his name was Kingsley, and determined to make his acquaintance, but that had to wait as the man left before Rory finished his meal.

Rankin also excused himself to attend to some piece of business or other, leaving Rory alone with Roper, Goodyear and M.M. as they lingered over coffee. It was Miles Roper who raised the question of their presence on the ship.

"I still can't understand why Duncan insisted on dragging us along on this jaunt. It seems crazy to me."

"He said it was in case of problems with the T2, and for our own safety, in case whoever murdered Paul and Norman tried to have a go at one of us," Goodyear reminded him.

"Murdered?" Rory burst out.

"Oh dear," Goodyear said, pulling a face. "I think I may have just broken the Official Secrets Act."

"I don't suppose it matters now," Wilson said calmly. "Yes, Rory me old mate. I'm afraid it's true. The suicide report was a cover-up to buy time. Poor old Paul and Norman were killed."

So his suspicions were not only correct, but Duncan had known all along. Rory felt irrationally angry with his Chief. Okay, so Rory had a lower security clearance than the scientists. But if only Duncan had known the implications – not least of which was that one of these three men was now an accessory to murder.

"The assumption is," Goodyear was saying, "that whoever did it is after the T2. But if that is the case they've obviously failed. There's no way anybody's going to lift it now."

"Which only makes it more irrational wanting us along," Roper persisted. "Once it was safely on board we could have gone back to Lairig and got on with our work. And as for our safety, we'd have been just as safe there, especially with the Highlanders in the place."

"I have a theory about that," Goodyear said thoughtfully.

"Oh?" Rory's eyebrows arched.

"Well there are two possibilities, actually. The most likely one is he thinks it's one of us."

"What is?" Roper asked, bewildered.

"Who's after the T2."

Roper shook his head disconcertedly. He had a brilliant brain, but like many such organs it was finely tuned to his rather narrow specialist field, outside which it could be surprisingly limited.

"But if he'd suspected one of us the last thing he would do is bring us along. He'd want us as far away from it as possible."

"Not if he hoped to catch the culprit red handed," M.M. suggested.

"Exactly." Goodyear seemed pleased that someone was keeping up with his thought process.

"I wouldn't put that past him," Rory agreed. "But what was the other possibility?"

"That Duncan himself is the culprit," Goodyear replied evenly. "After all, it was him who insisted on this trip."

"But then why bring us along?" Roper asked, shaking his small, neat head.

"He'd have no choice. If we hadn't come there would have been no reason for him to. And if he had manufactured an excuse, he would have been the only suspect. He'd have been clamped in irons the moment the theft was discovered."

Rory was looking vaguely at M.M. as this hypothesis was being expounded.

"But can you believe that of Duncan? That he is a terrorist?" he said vehemently. "Because I can't."

The question was directed at no-one in particular, but he was still looking at M.M., and it was he who answered.

"So which of us do you think does fit the bill, Rory? Me? Miles? Anthony? Which of us do you think has the right qualifications?"

Rory knew the question was unanswerable. All three men were his friends, and the idea that one of them had colluded in the deaths of Skinner and Dobbs, not to mention the attack on Rory himself, was ludicrous. Except for the fact that it almost certainly had to be true.

So which one did he plump for?

M.M.? Safe, amusing, avuncular entertainer and friend of little children? Whatever else it could not be him.

Miles Roper? The small, fastidious academic, who's mind was usually too preoccupied with scientific matters to know what was going on around him, and whose weakness for Dundee United was one his few points of contact with normal mortals? Apart from anything else it seemed unlikely that he would have been physically capable of the attack back at Lairig. And while he might be at home with hugely complex, multi-million pound scientific apparatus, if Rory had been a gambling man he would have laid a hefty wager that he would be unable to drive a tractor.

And that left Anthony Goodyear.

It would certainly be easier for an outsider to cast him in the role, on superficial grounds. He was younger than the others, and he had the

106

physique, and his luxuriant red beard and matching ponytail suited him perfectly for the role of Bluebeard's brother Ginger, but Rory knew the man underneath. He was a genuine gentle giant, who spoke softly and laughed often. He was without a temper - or at least Rory had never known him lose it - and as for being an accessory to murder, the man was a vegetarian, for heaven's sake.

Rory shook his head as he replied to Charlie Wilson's question.

"I know. It's ludicrous, isn't it."

"Not really. No." Goodyear said cheerfully. "Terrorists have an annoying habit of going around looking like everybody else. They don't grow horns, and more often than not when they are exposed their friends and neighbours - even family - are gobsmacked. How often have you seen them on telly saying: "I can't believe it. He was the quietest, nicest person you could imagine. He wouldn't hurt a fly."

"That's not true of the villains I've known," Rory protested. "As a P.C. I'd say ninety pert cent of the people I arrested very much looked the part. Complete tow-rags most of them."

"Yes. But they were mainly small time crooks, no doubt, involved in relatively minor larcenies. I am talking about a different class of person all together.

"Take the Krugers, or Philby, Maclean, Burgess, Blunt - pillars of the establishment. Even colleagues in MI5 didn't suspect anything for ages. Because they were not ogres. They were people of conscience doing what they believed was right. And taking huge personal risks in doing so. Even betraying your friends isn't necessarily a sign of wickedness or indifference. It can be an act of courageous self-sacrifice if you do it, reluctantly, for a noble purpose. If one believes passionately in a cause, whether it's a religion or a political point of view or animal rights or whatever, it is a sign of moral strength, not weakness, to pursue it regardless of the costs to oneself.

"Personally I believe any of us, or Duncan, or you for that matter, have the moral fibre necessary to be such a person."

M.M. laughed. "Your most delightful feature, Tony, is that we can always rely on you to come up with a fresh point of view. 'The terrorist as hero!'

"But of course you are right. Is does only depend on which side of the fence you are on as to what is heroism and what is an atrocity."

107

"Incidentally," Goodyear said, addressing Rory. "I only included you in the list out of politeness. You are in fact excused as a suspect since you were not invited on the trip, and are only here as a last minute substitute."

"Well thank you for the vote of confidence!" Rory replied sardonically. "I'm honoured."

"Joking apart though," M.M. said, "Tony's quite right. It could be any of us - or Duncan - and we can't get away from the fact."

There followed a long, and none too comfortable silence.

"Well that was a conversation stopper!" Goodyear grinned.

"It is a most uncomfortable situation," Miles Roper said earnestly.

"Especially," Rory put in, "Since you say that Dr. Skinner and Dr. Dobbs were murdered. You realise that whoever it is is implicated in that?"

"Yes," Goodyear agreed. "It's that which makes it so unreal. I know I am right in what I say about serving a cause you believe in, but I find it just as hard as you do to accept that one of us could have been involved in that.

"It's funny, isn't it. Stealing something capable of killing millions of people, and presumably being prepared to use it; that I can come to terms with. But Norman and Paul.... That's something quite different."

. . .

In the days that followed Rory began to learn first hand the truth of Rankin's comments about the boredom of life at sea. Not being part of the ship, time hung even more heavily on the hands of the passengers: at least the crew had their duties to perform, their watches and routines. Rory did not have enough to do, and it was not a situation he was used to.

The crew were friendly enough, though on the two occasions he saw the Captain he was greeted with a polite but short: "Good morning to you." And when Anthony Goodyear asked if there were any fishing rods on board with which he could do a bit of spinning, he was told there were, but they could not be used at sea as Captain North would not approve. "He feels it demeans the ship to use her as a fishing boat. We keep the rods for when we're in port."

The scientists had brought work with them, and Rory had some books, but reading and crosswords can only fill up so much of a day. He played pool with the crew and attended keep fit classes and watched videos and visited Duncan, but still he felt pent up and frustrated. The subtle tension of waiting and wondering who would contact him, and when, did not help. He had forgiven Duncan, but now he had even more questions to ask him as soon as he was on his feet again.

On the third day he was wandering about the ship at a loose end when he came upon the elusive Mr. Kingsley sitting alone at the wardroom bar, and seized the opportunity to make his acquaintance. If he was The Voice's man it would do no harm to make himself known.

"Good afternoon," Rory said, extending his hand. "I'm Rory Kilbride."

"Afternoon, Mr. Kilbride. Laurence Kingsley." He took Rory's hand in a firm grasp. "I've met your colleagues, the three scientists. They're an interesting trio."

"Yes. I'm escorting them to Johnston," Rory replied. "And what brings you on this trip?"

"I'm an engineer. I'm going to look at one of the incinerators. They're having trouble with the secondary burners."

"Wouldn't it have been quicker to fly out?"

"Infinitely, but I can't stand aeroplanes. Dreadful fear of flying, I'm afraid."

"But you don't mind ships? You're not getting bored to death?"

"Not at all. I've got your Dr. Wilson to entertain me for one thing. He's terrific with those conjuring tricks."

"Yes, he's good fun. Ideal person to have on a trip like this."

"Absolutely. Mind you the others seem like interesting characters too."

"They are. Dr. Goodyear is one of the world's top chemists, although he doesn't look like it. He's also a chess Grand Master, and plays the saxophone. Sickeningly talented, in fact. And yet he's a really nice person: very down-to-earth." He did not add that he could also be a kidnapper and murderer.

"That was my impression. And I gather he's into alternative medicine."

"Yes. He gets a lot of stick over that."

"What about Dr. Roper? Is he a friend of yours too? You seem to be a very non-hierarchical organisation."

"We are. It's historical. Probably to do with the fact that we are so isolated. And yes, I get on well with Miles too. We both support Dundee United. We sometimes go to matches together."

"And I believe there's another in your party who is indisposed." Was this polite small talk, or was Kingsley fishing like mad?

"Yes, my boss, Duncan McLennan. He's very seasick."

"He has my sympathy. It must be terrible."

Rory agreed that seasickness was a great affliction, and the conversation continued for nearly an hour, though for most of the time it was more like fencing than chatting. Kingsley gave away very little about himself, quickly and skilfully closing any conversational openings which Rory tried to create into his world, while at the same time subtly prodding away at Rory. He showed no interest in the work or security arrangements at Lairig, but seemed greatly curious about the individuals as people. In normal circumstances Rory would have been easily able to hold his own, and either face the other down or simply tell him to mind his own business. But the circumstances were not normal, and part of Rory hoped that if he gave the right answers this man might declare himself to be the one who held Hannah's fate in his hands.

But he did not, and when they finally parted Rory was unsure whether he had been expertly grilled, or had an innocent conversation with a man who liked a bit of gossip. It had not felt entirely innocent, though that could possibly be put down to his state of mind. Mr. Kingsley did not look like an engineer, or come across as a man who would be afraid of flying, but then as he himself had pointed out a number of times, Anthony Goodyear didn't look like a top-flight scientist, and anyone meeting M.M. for the first time would not take him for one either.

It took over a week for Duncan to find his sea legs. The colour was beginning to return to his face, and he was keeping small quantities of food down. One more day, Rory decided, and he will be well enough for a heart to heart.

That night Rory could not sleep. The tension, the boredom and the heat - they were now well into the Tropic of Cancer - all conspired against his normal ability to drop off the minute his head hit the pillow. He had gone to bed at eleven thirty, and tossed and turned for an hour before getting up and taking a shower.

But to no avail. By three o'clock he was still no nearer his goal, and giving up the struggle he dressed and went for a walk on deck. It was a dark night, there was no moon, but the ship was well lit up. With nothing particular in mind he climbed the ladder to the flight deck, and walked slowly astern. Below him the quarterdeck was less well illuminated, but he could make out the shapes of two figures standing shoulder to shoulder at the taffrail. They appeared to be deep in conversation as they took it in turn to lean across and shout in each others ear. Standing where they were, directly above the twin screws which were thrusting the four and a half thousand ton ship through the water, it must even then have been very hard to hear. It struck Rory as a strange place to hold a conversation when you had the whole of the ship to choose from, but perhaps sailors took it in their stride.

He was about to move on when the shorter of the two men began to finger his earlobe in a way which caught Rory's attention. It was exactly what Duncan did when he was thinking. Rory strained his eyes. Surely it could not be Duncan out there at that time of night? He was not off his sick bed yet, even if he was recovering.

As his eyes became accustomed to the dark, so the figure came more and more to resemble his Chief. The size and shape, and the movements and mannerisms were all familiar.

But if it was Duncan, who was he talking to? The other man was taller and somewhat thinner, and had blond or white hair, but Rory could not see any more than that. It did not look like any of the scientists. Intrigued, he watched for several minutes while the two men continued their strange, inaudible conversation. When they finally stopped and turned, Rory instinctively stepped back into the shadow of the hangar. He had no particular reason to avoid a meeting with Duncan: it was simply an automatic reaction.

111

As the two men walked towards him they crossed through the beam of one of the deck lights, and for the first time Rory saw their faces. He was right. It was Duncan.

And his companion was none other than Mr. Laurence Kingsley.

CHAPTER 6

Richard Warrender pulled the Range Rover to a halt in front of one of Strachan Manor's large stone mullion windows, and cast a proprietorial eye over the place. It had been a good purchase. The solid stone edifice was within reasonable reach of London, and yet sufficiently isolated to have no neighbour problems. It was large and old, but not old enough or interesting enough to be listed, or on anyone's agenda of places to visit. It was an ideal place for the Battalions of Gaia to own, as he had realised the moment he saw it four years previously. Not that there was any record of the purchase in the organisation's accounts.

It was a place where people could vanish without trace almost indefinitely, and thanks to the modifications which had been made even the most thorough search would not discover their whereabouts. The house was alerted as soon as a caller broke the beam at the gate, and was identified by closed circuit television. By the time they had made their way up the drive, slowed to a crawl by the pea gravel, deliberately laid wheel-spinningly deep, any occupant who felt the need could be safely in the suite of three interconnected rooms to which there was no detectable access, and whose presence would only be betrayed by a full architectural survey. These rooms contained sufficient rations for several months.

And then, of course, there was the cellar, with its own particular secret.

As Warrender climbed out of the Range Rover, Jonathan Howarth appeared at the front door and came to greet him.

"Nice to see you," Howarth said warmly.

"And you. Everything under control?"

"Yes. No problems."

"Good." Warrender followed him into the house and through to the large sitting room, comfortably if sparsely furnished in a style befitting a dignified but ageing country house.

Howarth offered his guest a fruit juice. He knew he would not want tea, coffee or alcohol, choosing to take into his body only fresh and natural nutrients. It was part of a regime to keep himself in the peak of physical and mental condition, whereby the better to serve the Cause.

Although he did not go quite so far himself, Howarth's own research into the subtle vagaries of the food chain had given him plenty of cause for concern. As one of the Government's leading scientific advisers he had been among the first to look into the relationship between BSE in cattle and CJD in humans, and he had found some very disturbing things. When he had tried to make these things public, however, he suddenly ceased to be a Government adviser, leading or otherwise, and the only way he could voice his concerns was through unofficial channels. He found the Battalions of Gaia a receptive and willing audience, but his previous employers did not take kindly to this either. He began to find himself the object of unwanted attention, convinced that his phone was being tapped, and that probably his mail was being interfered with too. His homosexuality, previously only his own business, suddenly and mysteriously became public knowledge, and when his house was burgled for the second time he turned to a new friend, Richard Warrender who, though not a member of the Battalions of Gaia, seemed to be a sympathiser. He was also a man with considerable contacts, and once convinced that Howarth's conversion was complete and uncompromising, arranged for him to disappear.

One night a removal van had arrived at his house, and he and his entire home had been shipped to a remote farmhouse on the Scottish border. A new identity had been supplied, and he was able to live and study in peace, amused to read the few column inches which the newspapers devoted to his disappearance.

He was contacted by a man named Carpenter with whom he soon became good friends. Initially he knew only that Gordon was a friend of Richard Warrender, though he came to suspect that they were involved in militant action of some kind. This did not disturb him as it might once have done. Having been on the receiving end of the Establishment's dirty tricks department he increasingly saw no reason for those who opposed the forces of Terracide to play by the rule book. He was greatly influenced by Gordon's reading of the environmental balance sheet, and in due course became a firm believer. Gordon apparently conveyed this to Warrender, and Howarth was asked if would be prepared to make another move, and take up residence at Strachan Manor. He would be housed and fed and receive

114

a small stipend, in return for which he had only to manage the house and its two staff - one of whom, the housekeeper, was currently out of the country - and be prepared to entertain the occasional guest. Given that all he wanted was anonymity and the chance to work, the arrangement could not have suited him better.

He had been more than a little disconcerted when his first 'guest' had turned out to be a young woman who arrived bound and gagged, but Warrender had explained the need, and assured Howarth that no harm was intended towards her. She was to be treated well, and given anything within reason which she asked for.

"So how is she?" Warrender asked, sipping his grape juice, and showing a degree of solicitude he did not feel. It was for Howarth's sake, not the girl's.

"She seems to have settled in okay. Here, I'll show you." Howarth picked up a sender unit from the coffee table, and as he pressed a button horse racing appeared on a television set in the corner of the room. He punched in a four digit combination, and the excitement of Chepstow was replaced by the view of the back of a young woman as she sat at a desk writing. "She was worried about getting behind with her studies, so I got her some books she wanted."

"Well done." Warrender stared at the screen for several thoughtful seconds. "And the phone call? It obviously did the trick."

"Yes. I got Carl to make it. He only has to say 'good morning' to put the frighteners on people. We had two follow-up calls because Kilbride wanted to get someone out of the way. I sent him what he needed, and I didn't hear any more till Gordon rang and told me he had caught the boat. What does he have to do exactly?"

"Kilbride? Not necessarily anything. As you know we have our own man on the ship. Rory is just an insurance policy. He's fit and competent, he can handle himself and he's an insider. We've just put him there in case he's needed. If all goes well our man will handle it himself, and Rory will go home wondering what all the fuss was about."

"And presumably Hannah too. What about the fact that she knows our faces?"

"No-one she's seen has a criminal record, so what is she going to do? Go round with the police knocking on every door in the country?"

115

And there's no need to kill her, Richard thought to himself. Once the world gets a taste of T2 looking for a bunch of kidnappers will be the last thing on anyone's mind.

"Fair enough. So what's the plan?"

"Once we have the chemical in our hands we can pretty well ask what we want. Gordon has drawn up a list of demands." Warrender explained the end to car production, the changes to the tax regime and the re-convening of the Earth Summit. He did not mention his variation of the plan.

"That's brilliant. And it might work. Just think of it: politicians actually having to produce results for once, instead of hot air."

"We seem to be heading in the right direction."

"What about the other group who are after it? The ones who killed the two scientists? Have you heard any more about them?"

"Not a word. They seem to have started the ball rolling and then dropped out of the picture. It's rather worrying frankly."

"Perhaps the security arrangements defeated them."

"Perhaps."

"Are you thinking they may still try something?"

"Why not? We are." Warrender pointed out reasonably. "That's one reason for wanting backup on the Lysander."

"Fair enough. Any idea then how much longer Hannah will be staying with us? She keeps asking."

"Couple of weeks. Three at the outside, and then you can tell her we'll be running her home."

"I will," Howarth told him. "She'll be pleased to hear that."

. . .

Rory knocked on the door of Duncan's cabin, and entered. Whatever state Duncan was in he was going to have a serious heart-to-heart, and it was not the one he had originally envisaged.

"Good morning Rory." Duncan was sitting up in bed. He was certainly a more healthy colour.

"Good morning." Rory's greeting was guarded; less enthusiastic than his Chief's. "How do you feel?"

"Much better, thanks. Positively human, in fact."

116

"I thought you must do."

Duncan raised an interrogatory eyebrow. "How's that?"

Rory tried to keep it casual, but it came out as an accusation. "Wandering about the deck in the middle of the night?"

"You were awake too, were you? I suppose it's the heat. Though I've been in bed so long it's no wonder I can't sleep."

"And who was your friend?"

"Friend? I bumped into a chap called Kingsley, if that's what you mean. Is that a problem?" The edge in Rory's voice was not lost on Duncan.

"Strange place to bump into someone, let alone hold a conversation. It must be rather hard to hear above that noise."

Duncan eyed Rory as though weighing up whether to humour him or chew him off a strip for insubordination. "I was wandering round the ship, and he happened to be there. I suppose he couldn't sleep either. We had a chat out of politeness, but nothing that warranted looking for somewhere quieter."

Rory cast his mind back over the scene of the previous night. It had not looked like a casual chat. It looked like a serious discussion, held where it could not be overheard.

"I understand the deaths of Dr. Skinner and Dr. Dobbs were not suicide," he said abruptly.

Duncan's eyebrows went back up. "Someone's been talking out of turn."

"It was one of the boffins. It was an accident. They assumed I already knew."

"What else did they tell you?" Rory noted that he did not ask who had made the gaffe.

"Nothing I didn't already know. I suppose it's the same person who attacked me at Lairig?"

"That's a fair working assumption."

Rory decided to put Goodyear's theory to the test.

"And you think it's one of the boffins, and that's why you brought them along?"

Duncan smiled.

"That's very perceptive."

Rory did not admit that it had not been his idea.

"You really think one of them would kill Skinner and Dobbs? They were all friends."

"Not personally. Apart from anything else none of them left Lairig that night. And I don't want to believe it any more than you do, laddie, but we have to face the facts as we know them.

"Have you any idea which one it might be?"

"None at all."

"Or why they would want to steal the T2?"

"Absolutely none."

"You don't think they'll still try anything, do you? Not here?" Rory made a vague gesture which encompassed the ship. "They have everything from small arms to Exocet missiles on this thing, by way of a Westland helicopter. Not to mention a well trained crew of nearly three hundred."

Duncan shrugged. "I like to keep an open mind."

"And that is why I am here? As backup?"

"That's about it."

"Then why on earth didn't you tell me earlier?"

"You know how the game is played, Rory. Strictly on a need to know basis. You didn't need to know, and you still don't for that matter. I should have filled you in as soon as the dung looked as though it was about to hit the rotor blades. But since you are now in the picture you can keep your eyes peeled and your mouth shut."

"Naturally."

"And I'll tell you something else. It's grand to feel well again. I think I am going in search of the world's largest breakfast."

"Then I'll leave you to dress." Rory headed for the door, then stopped and turned. "What did you make of Mr. Kingsley, by the way?"

Duncan grinned. "Difficult to say really. I could hardly hear a word he said."

And that, thought Rory as he closed the door behind him, was a very neat piece of evasion.

. . .

At eleven o'clock the following evening Rory became aware of a change in the note of the engines, and was informed by the midshipman with whom he was playing cribbage that they would be approaching the Panama canal. He went up on deck, and for the first time in eleven days looked out and saw land. The big warship slowed, and eventually dropped anchor half a mile from an oil tanker, which lay, lit overall, awaiting her turn to pass through the canal.

Rory savoured the tantalising sight of the lights of the port of Colón in the distance, but his companion informed him that they would not now be entering the canal until first light, and in due course they returned to their cards.

At 03.37 hrs, the ship's main broadcast woke Rory as the speaker in the corner of his cabin came insistently to life.

"Attention all hands. This is the Captain. I am placing the ship on Condition Orange. Repeat Orange. Medical detail to the armoury, immediate. Commander Ussher, helicopter crew and yeoman of signals to bridge. All crew to action stations. Accommodation ladder and launch to be prepared for immediate use. This is not, repeat not, an exercise. Message ends."

Rory grabbed some clothes, threw them on, and opened his door. Outside the ship was alive as people, in various states of attire, raced along the passageway in both directions. As a rating he knew went past Rory tried to ask him what was happening, but the man either did not hear or did not have time to stop.

Rory ran down the passageway to his left, and out onto the deck. He looked out to sea, half expecting to find the Lysander was under attack. All he could see, however, were purposeful groups of sailors going about their business. From somewhere above him powerful spotlights were beaming out into the night, criss-crossing each other as they quartered the inky surface of the sea, and to his left a detail were working the davits which supported a powerful looking launch. Everyone was fully absorbed in their work, and in the hope of finding someone less occupied who might have the time to tell him what was going on, he turned right and began to climb the ladder to the flight

119

deck.

As he reached the top he was confronted by the feet of a Petty Officer.

"I'm sorry sir," the man said, looking down at him, "but you can't come up here just at the moment."

Rory stopped climbing, his eyes level with the deck. "What's going on?"

"The ship's been placed on Condition Orange, sir. That is one step down from full battle stations, so you'd best be getting back to your cabin. You're liable to get in someone's way otherwise."

"Yes, but what has happened?"

"'Fraid I can't tell you that sir."

Rory was suddenly aware of what it felt like to be an outsider. Not just to be useless, but worse than useless. Something that might 'get in someone's way'. He was used to being the one in control. At Lairig, and before that in the police force, he was the one in authority, the one ordering people around and keeping the public out of the way. He did not like the experience of being on the other side of the fence.

Reluctantly he climbed back down the ladder and began to make his way aft. As he did so he was intercepted by another of the ship's officers.

"Captain's compliments sir. He would like you to come to the wardroom. If you would follow me."

Rory did not bother to protest that he knew the way. He had no objection to being escorted, and with luck the others would be there too and they would be told what was going on.

The others were not there, but they arrived very soon, each personally escorted by a member of the crew. Miles Roper was the last of the Lairig contingent to arrive, striped pyjamas visible beneath his green and tartan dressing gown, his unlit pipe clenched between his teeth.

No sooner had he entered the room than they were joined by another officer whom Rory had seen from time to time in the mess. He was a tall man, slightly stooped, and older than most of the crew. He looked around the assembled company, and seemed dissatisfied. After a few moments Laurence Kingsley was escorted protesting into the room, and the tall man seemed to relax.

"Good morning gentlemen. My name is Larkin," he introduced himself. "I am the third officer. The Captain has asked me to appraise you of our current circumstances." He talked the way schoolteachers were supposed to have done a century ago. "Something unfortunate has occurred, as you may have surmised from the commotion on the ship.

"A short while ago a seaman was discovered in the passageway near the armoury, having apparently been the victim of an assault. The man has head wounds, and is currently unconscious.

"It seems that he came upon his injuries as a result of surprising a person or persons in the act of opening the armoury door with an oxyacetylene burner."

He paused for a moment, and looked forlornly at Duncan. I regret to say. Mr. McLennan, that your canister is missing."

"What!" Duncan erupted to his feet, both fists striking the table as he rose.

Larkin raised his hand. "Please. I do understand that the contents are of a sensitive nature."

Duncan shook his head in disbelief, and Larkin continued seriously: "Everything possible is being done to trace the missing article, and an immediate sea search has been launched. We are working on the assumption that the perpetrators came aboard by stealth, and have made off with it." He put his fist to his mouth, and cleared his throat.

"We also have to make the assumption that they had assistance from someone on board. They knew what they wanted, where it was, and where the ship's workshop is." He looked embarrassed. "They used one of our own acetylene cutters."

At this point a young officer-in-training appeared in one of the doorways and looked round the assembled company. "Is Mr. McLennan here?"

Duncan turned to him. "I'm McLennan."

"The Captain would like to see you on the bridge sir. Right away. If you would follow me."

Duncan followed the sailor to the bridge, where seven men were responding to the emergency with cool, unflustered efficiency. Captain North was addressing two men in flying overalls who had entered the bridge seconds before Duncan and his escort.

"We have an injured man aboard," he told them. "The medical detail should have him up on the flight deck any time. He needs to go to Panama, Colón doesn't have the facilities." He handed them a fax. "Here's the signal we received from the hospital. It gives the coordinates and explains where you are to land."

"Very good sir." One of the men took the piece of paper, and they left at a fast jog.

North then turned to another officer. "The launch should be ready by now, Bill. It'll have to be a rough and ready search. I would imagine you're looking for something small and dark - possibly a canoe even. Best of luck."

"Thanks. It sounds as though we'll need it."

When he had left, North turned to Duncan.

"As Mr. Larkin has told you, your cargo has been stolen. I know it was a metal cylinder, I have seen the others in the paint store. What was inside it?"

"A glass phial - about nine inches high. Holds a pint, though this one is only half full of a greenish liquid."

North returned to Russell. "Right, so that's what we're looking for. I want you to put together four search parties, and go over the ship from stem to stern. Look for anything suspicious, but particularly a metal cylinder or a glass phial. There are four of them in the paint store, have a look at one before you begin. And then start the search with the passengers' cabins.

Duncan gave an involuntary snort. "I don't know how that will go down," he said. "You are talking about three eminent scientists who are not used to having their privacy invaded."

"Then they shouldn't hitch lifts on my ship," North returned. "But in the name of public relations I will come down and explain the situation in person. He glanced round the bridge, checking that everything was under control. "You okay here for a few minutes number one?"

Commander Ussher nodded.

"Let's go then." North led the way back to the ward room.

"Good morning," he greeted the assembled company. "You know the nature of the problem. I want to assure you that I am doing everything in my power to retrieve the missing article. As well as a sea search - we believe someone has been aboard and may be escaping in a small boat - I am having the ship searched overall. While that is being undertaken I must ask you to remain here. Your belongings will, of course, have to be included in the search."

"What!" Eyebrows were raised all round, but it was Miles Roper who responded most vehemently. "You can't do that! It's a gross invasion of privacy. I will not allow it."

"I am afraid it is necessary."

Roper rose to his feet. "We'll see about that." He made for the door, but as he did so a burly leading seaman stepped sideways and blocked his path. Roper stopped at the human wall, his empty pipe quivering in his hand. "Let me pass," he demanded, but when the wall refused to budge he turned to North. "This is unlawful imprisonment. I shall sue!" His voice was at least an octave higher than usual, and he was now shaking from head to toe.

Captain North shook his head very slightly. "Aboard this ship I am the law. If you have something to hide, doctor, this would be a good time to tell me about it. Otherwise you will wait here until you are told you may leave."

North returned to the bridge, and Larkin and Russell went about their business too, but not before two men had been stationed at each of the doorways. Miles had stalked back to his chair, where he huddled, sucking his pipe noisily, suppressed anger radiating from him like neutrons from a fusion reactor.

Rory had watched his friend's display of temper with some amazement. It was out of character, and out of all proportion to the circumstances. Rory did not like the situation either, but he could accept that he too was under suspicion as far as Captain North was concerned, as were all the others. And the way to allay that fear was not by ranting and threatening legal action. He watched Roper unobtrusively for a long time, wondering just what was making him so upset.

Goodyear and Wilson seemed calm enough. Anthony Goodyear had availed himself of reading material, as had Duncan, from the officers' library, and M.M. found a comfortable chair and was soon sleeping soundly. Miles eventually calmed down enough to select a magazine, but Rory suspected he was not really reading it, merely using it as something to hide behind.

Why did he take such an exception to having his cabin searched? He was by nature a private man; was it simply that he could not stand the idea of another person going through his belongings? Rory had come across people like that in his police days, reacting emotionally - even violently - to having their homes searched, even though they proved to have nothing to hide.

The search of the ship seemed to go on for ever, and for Rory at least, being pent up, useless, in that wardroom was like a sentence to one of the less salubrious levels of purgatory. He still found it hard to accept that one of the boffins was apparently prepared to sell his secrets, assault Rory himself, and be a party to kidnap and murder. He thought back over as many of his conversations with each of them as he could remember, racking his brains for any inconsistency, hint of a clue, and was still doing so when Captain North re-entered the room.

He looked around his five passengers, his eyes settling momentarily on Miles, who appeared to shrink beneath his gaze. For a moment Rory suspected he was close to tears.

"The ship," North said, addressing the room at large, "has now been searched from thoroughly. I regret to say that the missing canister has not been found."

"You didn't find anything?" Anthony Goodyear asked.

"No. That is not quite true. We found these." North held up a small collection of pamphlets. Rory could read the title of the front one: 'Terricide - the killing of a planet'. "They are environmentalist publications. I should describe them as being of an extreme nature."

"Where did you find them?" M.M. asked, but it was not Captain North who answered him: it was Duncan McLennan.

"In my cabin."

"Indeed." North turned his heavily-browed eyes on him, and everyone else in the room followed suit. "A fact which I feel requires some explanation."

"You should not." If Duncan felt any sense of unease it did not show. "Is it not one of the first principles of warfare that you should know your enemy? I am sure you follow that principle, Captain. The people who produce these pamphlets are my enemy, and so I study

124

them."

"I see." Captain North shuffled the documents in his hands, looking with distaste at the various titles: 'Global warming. The point of no return.' 'Gaia. The death of a Goddess?' With a snort he dropped them on the table in front of Duncan.

Rory listened to the exchange with a sense of unreality. It was the first he had heard of environmentalists. In fact Duncan had told him less than twenty-four hours ago that he had no idea who they were up against. He was tempted to challenge him with the discrepancy then and there, but his loyalty to Duncan ran deep, and he owed it to him to settle this man to man; not here in public. The most he could be guilty of, after all, was playing his cards too close to his chest, and this would be for a very good reason.

"So where do we go from here?" Duncan asked North. "An extremely dangerous and secret substance, for which I am responsible, has disappeared. I have allowed you your search of the ship, but since that has drawn a blank I think we shall have to start working together."

Rory expected a minor explosion from North and was surprised by his response. "Those tracts place a large question mark over your head as far as I am concerned, Mr. McLennan, but while it remains only a question mark I am prepared to give you the benefit of the doubt. You are wrong about one thing, however. While your canister was on my ship it was my responsibility. And I am responsible for its loss. No-one else."

Whatever else you might say about Captain North, Rory thought to himself, many a cabinet minister could learn a thing or two from him about accepting responsibility.

It was a thought which occurred to Duncan too. "It's not a matter of whose fault it was, Captain," he said appreciatively. "The only question that matters is how we get it back."

"The launch is still out looking. Of course we could do a much more thorough search by helicopter, but I was only allocated one for this trip, and that is taking the injured man ashore.

"During the search of the ship a pool of water was found up for'ard by the port anchor chain, which suggests skin divers may have come aboard. If that is the case, and they got away under water, I'm afraid we may have to face the fact that you will not see the canister again."

The three scientists and Duncan looked at each other in a shared horror. "Shouldn't we tell him?" Anthony Goodyear asked.

"Tell me what?" North queried.

Duncan flashed a 'no' to Goodyear with his eyes, then turned to North. "There is nothing that you don't already know. The material in the canister is very, very dangerous. Considerably worse than Sarin or Tabun or any of the conventional chemical war agents. That is the reason for our presence here which, as you know, was sanctioned by the Minister of Defence in person. If it falls into...." He paused before correcting himself. "If it has fallen into the wrong hands, the prospects are appalling. I cannot emphasise that enough."

North nodded. "I understand. I have ordered the chopper to begin a search of the shoreline on its was back from Panama, and to continue for as long as its fuel holds out. I have also alerted the civilian authorities, and they are putting out patrol boats. Beyond that I don't know what more we can do tonight, other than pray." He cast an eye round the room. "Though the fact remains that whoever has taken the thing away had help from someone on board. I take it no-one has anything to tell me on that account?"

Nobody did.

"Very well. You have the freedom of the ship."

After North left the wardroom emptied quickly; they had all been in there quite long enough. Charlie Wilson and Anthony Goodyear left together, followed closely by Miles Roper and then Duncan. Rory followed Duncan out onto the deck, took his arm, and steered him firmly over to the rail.

"You never mentioned any environmentalists to me," he said without preamble. "When did they come into the picture?"

"I've known for some time that it was a possibility," Duncan replied evenly. "Information received from Scotland Yard. Anti-terrorist Branch."

"I see. And you didn't feel able to share this with me?"

"Nope. Apart from anything else, Rory, isn't your Hannah a bit strong in that department?"

Duncan might as well have hit him. The mention of Hannah's name came as a physical blow. And this was the first time Duncan had ever intimated that their relationship might compromise Rory's security standing.

So Duncan was not levelling with him because he did not trust him. And he no longer completely trusted Duncan. This could become very unpleasant indeed.

"Hannah's no terrorist," he said as lightly as he could. "She belongs to the Battalions of Gaia, but they're harmless enough." He paused. "Aren't they?"

"I imagine so," Duncan responded vaguely. "But you can never be totally sure of these things. What did you make of Miles' reaction to having his baggage searched?"

There was an evasion, if ever there was one, Rory thought. Deftly done as always. "It seemed extreme."

"That's what I felt. I half expected them to find the canister in his things."

Rory refrained from saying: 'instead of which they found your reading material,' and chose rather to say: "Yes. It would be interesting to know what that was all about. Are you going to ask him?"

"No point. If he's our man he's hardly going to tell us. He'd just say it was an invasion of privacy. He is, after all, a very private person. And they did not find anything."

"He still looked to me as though he expected them to."

"Me too. And I thought North gave him a rather old-fashioned look when he came back in. And neither of the other two looked at all worried about having their cabins searched."

Rory turned and studied his face. "Nor did you," he reminded him. "But you must have realised they would find those pamphlets, and that it would look damned suspicious."

"I've explained those," Duncan said easily. "I had nothing to feel guilty about. And Miles apparently did, and yet they didn't find it." He shook his head at the problem.

"Could somebody have moved it for him?"

"Where to? They searched the whole ship."

Rory thought. "What if they dropped it overboard, for the divers to pick up?"

"It's a possibility, I suppose. But who could have done it? We were

127

all herded up in the wardroom."

"What about Kingsley? He came in after the rest of us, and not long after Miles, as I recall."

"That's true. I suppose he might have had time to get to Miles' room and heave it out of the porthole." Duncan thought about it. "But how would he have known to? He'd have had no idea the ship was going to be searched until he had been taken to the wardroom, like the rest of us."

"That's true." They both fell into a thoughtful silence, and watched the rapid tropical coming of dawn.

It was full light when the helicopter returned, coming in low over the water like some huge, dark insect. Word soon went round the ship that they had found nothing, as had the launch and the civilian authorities. Official confirmation of this came just after eight on the ship's main broadcast.

"This is the Captain. Able seaman Frost is in hospital in Panama. He has concussion, but his condition is stable. I shall inform you as bulletins come in.

"The air and sea searches have been called off. They were unsuccessful.

"I should like to see Mr. McLennan on the bridge right away please.

"Message ends."

Duncan, who was back in his cabin catching up on his lost sleep, dressed and made his way up to the bridge. North straightened from the chart table and greeted him.

"Good morning. You heard the broadcast I take it."

"That's why I'm here."

"Quite. So you will have gathered that we found nothing. I'm afraid they got clean away."

Duncan nodded. "It's just an idea, but the canister couldn't have been dropped overboard?"

"I thought of it. Divers have been down, but they couldn't see it. Of course it could already have been picked up, but I have dropped a radio marker buoy, just in case."

"So that's about it."

128

"Looks like it. Needless to say I deeply regret this incident, but I do not see what more there is to be done. We have already missed our canal slot, and I shall have to take the next available one and continue on to Johnston as scheduled. But there is no reason now for you and your scientists to stay with us. I take it you will have no objection if I make arrangements to fly you home from Panama?"

"I don't see that there's any alternative," Duncan said unenthusiastically. "I take it you've informed the MoD?"

"Of course. And they are informing the security services. I'm sure they'll be putting their best men onto it. Now, when we can get you all on a flight I'll have you taken to the airport in the Westland."

CHAPTER 7

The first available flight to England did not leave for two days, and the Lairig contingent resigned themselves to the prospect of a further forty-eight hours afloat. As far as Rory was concerned, at least, there was little pleasure to be had from this. There was a certain sense of relief that he had not been called on to help with the theft, but that was more than offset by the fact that he was no nearer to knowing who had taken Hannah, and he could do nothing for her except pray that she would be released now her captors had what they wanted. Adding to this the fact that he had failed in his official task of protecting the T2, and that in all probability someone somewhere now had their hands on the most lethal substance known to man, he had little to feel pleased about.

And his relationship with Duncan was soured. Rory had finally, very reluctantly, come to accept that even Duncan could not be considered above suspicion. He had, he knew, been letting his personal feelings for his Chief cloud his judgement, and he could not simply overlook his midnight conversation with Kingsley. Or the pamphlets, so glibly explained. Or the fact that he was still fully dressed at three in the morning on the night that Rory had been attacked at Lairig.

Goodyear had been absolutely right in what he said about terrorists and traitors. They were exactly like everybody else.

And that raised the question of the evasive and enigmatic Laurence Kingsley.

The list of possible suspects was now up to five, and each widening of the field meant that he was that much further away than ever from identifying Hannah's kidnappers. The only consolation was that they would soon be on their way home, and his first act would be to phone the mobile number and ask about Hannah. Now they had what they wanted they would surely release her? What would they gain by harming her now?

He knew that this was a false assumption. It would depend on a whole host of things: who they were, whether they had killed before, whether Hannah was in a position to identify them.... But he had to hold onto something, or he would go mad with worry.

His reverie was interrupted by the ship's main broadcast. "Attention. This is the Captain. Mr. McLennan to the bridge immediately please. Repeat, Mr. McLennan to the bridge."

He might have imagined it, but he felt he detected an edge in Captain North's normally even and self-assured announcing voice. Rory headed towards Duncan's cabin. He was accustomed to being needed when there was a flap on, to take his place automatically at Duncan's shoulder ready to back up or receive orders; and old habits die hard.

He met Duncan at the head of the companionway from their deck, and fell in step beside him. "Sounds important," he suggested.

"Did rather, didn't it," Duncan agreed. "I'd invite you along, but North can be a bit stuffy about who goes onto his bridge." They reached the doorway. "Wait here, and you'll be the first to know what it's all about."

Rory had waited a mere three minutes when Duncan reappeared, looking considerably more thoughtful than when he went in. He shook his head in disbelief at Rory. "A group calling themselves the 'Popular Front for the Liberation of Planet Earth' have been in touch with the Ministry of Defence. They say they will start releasing T2 at undisclosed locations from tomorrow if their demands are not met."

"And what are they demanding?"

"So far only one thing." Duncan shook his head again. "That no-one boards, or disembarks from, the frigate *Lysander*."

"Why on earth...."

"No idea. No-one has. No-one knows any more than you and I do." He frowned. "I don't suppose the boffins are going to like it. They were looking forward to going home."

"So was I," Rory said vehemently.

"Captain North is not a happy man, either," Duncan continued. "To be receiving his orders from a bunch of terrorists is really giving him heartburn."

"I can imagine. And I sympathise. There's nothing worse than having to act with a gun to your head." And I should know, he thought bitterly.

He returned to his cabin to think. Normally he would have gone with Duncan and they would put their heads together, but things were no longer normal. He wondered, fleetingly, if they ever would be again.

For over an hour he turned matters over in his mind, examining the problem from every angle. But even allowing for the fact that he could not necessarily take Duncan at his word he could still not see how it made any sense. If those concerned - the 'Popular Front for the Liberation of Planet Earth', at least he now had a name for them - had what they wanted, why did they not want their man off the ship as soon as possible? Or was there someone else they wanted to keep out of the way? Or did they have some further mission for the *Lysander*? The possibilities were endless, but a coherent, rational explanation evaded him.

. . .

The first problem they encountered was that they could not go through the canal without a pilot on board. North signalled London for orders, and for several hours messages flew between the RN Headquarters in Northwood, the Ministry of Defence and Scotland Yard as negotiations were made with the 'PFLPE'. Eventually permission was given for a pilot to go on board, and the *Lysander* began her journey through the fifty mile canal.

Natural curiosity reinforced by the absence of anything to look at recently brought the Lairig contingent out onto the deck in force.

Once the pilot had come aboard and taken charge of the ship, they passed through the breakwater into Limón Bay and headed towards the great Gatun Locks. Along the eastern side of the bay the busy town of Cristóbal, with its docks and shipyards and fuelling station gave the sightseers plenty to look at. Once across the bay they arrived at the foot of the flight of locks that would use the power of water to lift them eighty-five feet up to the level of Gatun Lake, the vast inland waterway which the canal builders created by damming up the Chagres River, thereby reducing the actual digging required to the eight miles of the Gailland Cut.

Rory, standing between Miles Roper and Anthony Goodyear, watched as canal workers attached towing cables to the *Lysander* from small electric railway engines on each side of the lock. Once done the frigate began to creep forward, guided and assisted by the *mules*. The whole operation was completed with the effortless efficiency of skilled workers performing an endlessly rehearsed routine.

When they were safely and squarely in the lock the huge steel gates closed silently behind them and the ship slowly began to rise, lifted by the waters of Gatun Lake as they were fed into underwater sluices.

From his vantage point on the port rail Rory could see another ship, which looked like an oil tanker, making the opposite journey down towards them in the parallel flight.

Goodyear wandered across to the other side of the deck, and Roper and Rory followed in the aimless manner of men with too much time on their hands.

"It's a fantastic feat of engineering," Anthony Goodyear enthused.

"Mind boggling," Rory agreed.

"It cuts the journey from the east coast of the USA to the west by 8,000 miles," Roper put in. "It took ten years to build and collects 400 million dollars a year in tolls.

Rory grinned. "And employs 7,000 people to run it; mostly Panamanians." He had taken the same book out of the ship's library.

Goodyear nodded down towards a group of five men, four of whom were looking idly on as the fifth was picking away with a spade at a loose piece of concrete.

"And there is 0.07 per cent of them toiling away with the diligence and enthusiasm of the devoted artisan the world over. It's amazing how...."

The sentence was cut off by a loud explosion from the other side of the ship. The three men ran across the deck towards the plume of dark grey smoke that was billowing up into the still air.

Looking down at the base of the column it was clear the explosion had occurred at the bottom of one of the flights of steps which rise between the two flights of locks, inside the twin tracks on which the electric *mules* climb and descend steeply from one water level to another.

Mark Twain said that if your only tool is a hammer all your problems will look like nails. So it is that if your stock in trade is chemical weaponry, that will be the first thought that occurs at a

133

moment such as this. Exactly the same idea went through the minds of all three men, as it did with M.M. and Duncan McLennan who had appeared further along the deck. Was this why they had been told to continue their journey? Did that rising cloud contain T2 molecules? Was this a high profile demonstration of the newly acquired power of the PFLPE? There could certainly be nothing more calculated to disrupt international trade and catch the world's attention than putting the Panama Canal out of action by contaminating it with the deadly, invisible toxin.

The question remained unspoken. Each man knew the implications, and there was very little to be said. They would know the answer soon enough.

. . .

Major Tom Bowen leant on his shovel, affecting the nearest thing he could to a slouch. It did not come naturally to an officer of the Special Boat Service, the naval equivalent of the SAS, but his normal alert, erect posture did not sit well with the battered straw hat and clean but well worn workaday clothes he was wearing.

His skin too had changed, darkened with some makeshift dye to give him the natural tanned look of the native Panamanian.

The hat was good. It protected him from the sun and hid his short, fair hair, and the brow hid his face from anyone looking down from above. His four companions, all similarly disguised, were making a good fist of their role as a maintenance crew; men trying to look usefully employed while involving themselves in the minimum of actual physical effort.

While Piers Laughton, an electronic warfare expert and veteran of the Falklands War, picked away in a desultory manner at a loose patch of concrete, Tom risked a glance across at the *Lysander* which now stood motionless in the still water of the second of the three locks, just a few feet away from him.

Just forward of amidships a watertight door had been opened in her side, and inside two naval officers stood waiting, a rolled up rope ladder at their feet. Above them, on the deck, three men stood looking directly down at him. He lowered his head, spat vigorously into the canal, and returned his attention to Piers' latest efforts.

Everything was ready. Crossing his fingers that included Milo Wannamaker, he let go of his spade so that it fell to the floor.

It had not been a matter of luck, finding a US army explosives expert so close at hand. Fort Davis, where Milo was based, was only one of a number of American military installations along the Canal Zone, built and maintained to defend that most essential of strategic thoroughfares. With four forts, two air bases, and the US Southern Command to choose from, Major Bowen could have called on experts in any field of military expertise he needed.

But all he required to get him and his men onto the *Lysander* was a diversion. Something that would take the attention of everyone in the area for a few essential seconds. The genial, round-faced Wannamaker had grinned through his heavy, horn-rimmed glasses.

"I know exactly what you mean," he beamed. "Lots o' noise, lots o' pyrotechnics, no damage. Just a giant firecracker. Not a problem. We'll just pack a few goodies into an old gas drum and roll it down the steps when you say the word."

"We need it when the ship is stationary in the middle lock. I'll drop my spade when we're ready."

"Okeydoke. You drop your spade, we'll raise the roof. Just leave it to Uncle Milo."

And he was as good as his word. Less than ten seconds after Tom's spade hit the ground the explosion echoed round the locks. Even with the *Lysander* between him and it, Bowen was impressed by the noise. And it had exactly the desired effect. Every face for half a mile jerked automatically towards the source of the bang. Or rather every face but five. Tom and the other four soldiers were the exception. They dropped their tools and dived into the lock. As they swam underwater across to the frigate the ladder was dropped out of the open door by their reception committee. One after another they surfaced and climbed with practised ease up into the ship.

They were showering and changing before the smoke had finished billowing from the twisted wreck of the burnt out oil drum.

. . .

135

"What the hell do you think that was?" Charlie Wilson asked, moving along the rail to join Rory and his two companions.

"I've no idea. My first thought was a chemical attack," Miles replied.

"Yes. Mine too. But I assume it isn't. I think we'd know by now."

Searching for an answer they peered down at the scene below, where some of Milo's own men had appeared, and were appearing very thorough and efficient. Bystanders were kept away, operation of the two flights of locks was suspended for a token fifteen minutes, and the area of the explosion was cordoned off and guards posted.

Milo himself appeared and checked the wreckage, which he obviously proclaimed non-dangerous, for the *mules* were allowed to move again, the water flow, and the greatest man-made waterway in the world went back about its business.

Aboard the *Lysander* only a handful of people knew about the stowaways who were now hidden in a store room in the bowels of the ship.

Once out of the last lock the frigate continued on its way south into Gatun Lake and then south-east all the way to the Bay of Panama. From the deck the sightseers saw in the distance one of the hyacinth patrols at work, clearing the lake of the green and violet water hyacinths that floated in their millions, and which, if not kept under control, would wreak havoc as their tough stems wrapped themselves round the propellers of passing ships.

Later the lake narrowed, and after Gamboa they entered the Gaillard Cut; the eight mile stretch of true canal which was driven over a period of ten years through swamp and jungle by an army of men led by David Gaillard. Here work was under way to widen the the cut. Originally dug a mere fifty feet wide it permits only one way traffic - a severe limitation for a waterway used by over 12,000 ships a year.

Once clear of the cut more electric *mules* were waiting to assist them into the Pedro Miguel lock which lowered them into Miraflores Lake. After crossing the one and a half mile lake under their own power the Miraflores Locks finally lowered them to the level of the Pacific Ocean.

136

The pilot left them after they passed under the Thatcher Ferry Bridge which carries the Pan American Highway across the canal, and Captain North took control once again as they headed out towards the Flamenco Islands and the open sea.

CHAPTER 8

The bedside phone brought him out of a deep sleep, and Neville Thorpe stared groggily at the clock, trying to take in the fact that it was a quarter to five in the morning. He groped for the receiver and rolled onto his back to free his right ear.

"Yes?" he said tersely.

"Good morning, Minister. I am sorry to wake you." Dempster Forbes had probably never sounded sorry for anything in his life, and this was no exception. "Something has come up which requires your immediate personal attention. I have taken the liberty of ordering you a car."

"What is it?" Thorpe was not chatty at the best of times, and this hour could definitely be improved upon.

"I can't go into details on the phone, but Sir Trevor Peacock is on the way over here. Among others."

"When will the car be here?" If the head of SO13, Scotland Yard's anti-terrorist squad, was going to the Home Office at five in the morning the presence of the Home Secretary was scarcely optional.

"Ten minutes, Minister."

"I will be waiting."

Peacock was in fact the last to arrive, along with one of his staff; a Commander Robert Taylor. Before them Dempster Forbes, Thorpe's PPS, ushered into his room Geoffrey Bagnall, the Director General of MI5, one of his section heads by the name of Douglas Tierney, Rear Admiral Rupert Owens, who somehow arrived from Northwood before Thorpe did from Kensington, and Major General Hugo Browne of the Royal Marines.

As soon as the two policemen arrived the meeting got under way, and it was Admiral Owens who opened the proceedings.

"This is a tricky business, Minister. And as you can see it involves a number of different agencies. Hitherto it has been mainly a matter of defence, but now things have taken a bit of a turn. If I may fill you in on the background:

"Some weeks ago the Defence Research Establishment at Lairig a' Mhuic came up with a new, rather nasty type of chemical war agent.

From a strategic point of view the stuff was useless. Too toxic and long lasting. It could never have been used in a conflict situation. So it was loaded onto a frigate and sent to an incinerator in the Pacific to be destroyed.

"Unfortunately, half way there, it disappeared."

"Disappeared?" Neville Thorpe's repetition of the word invested it with a sense of implausibility and perfidy which was quite lacking in the original.

"Yes Minister. Unlikely as it seems, it appears to have been stolen. By terrorists."

It was unclear to the others in the room whether Thorpe was blaspheming or praying aloud as he turned his eyes briefly to the ceiling.

"I hope you are not about to tell me what I think you may be about to tell me, Admiral," he told his visitor.

"'Fraid I am," Owens continued, unfazed. "We then started receiving messages from a group calling themselves the Popular Front for the Liberation of Planet Earth. Environmentalists. Nutters. Said they'd got the stuff and would use it if we didn't do what they said."

"When was this?"

"Forty-eight hours ago."

"Why was I not informed then?"

"Not a Home Office matter, Minister. They and the ship were on the other side of the world. The MoD was kept fully informed."

"So why me now?"

"I'll get to that in just a minute. Thing is, all they wanted was for the frigate to continue on course. Obviously they had something in mind for it, and as it had to go through the Panama Canal we took the opportunity to put some marines on board. Five of our best men from the SBS.

"And then we received this." It was Sir Trevor Peacock who finished the story, handing a sheet of fax paper to Thorpe.

Thorpe read.

> 'Contrary to our instructions you have put five men aboard the *Lysander*. As a consequence our recent acquisition will be demonstrated in the London Underground within the week. The survival of Gaia is

139

paramount. The Popular Front for the Liberation of Planet Earth.'

"What is this last part?" Thorpe asked. "'The survival of Gaia is paramount.'"

"It's a code phrase. They put it on all their communications. Shows it's genuine."

"Hmph." Thorpe peered again at the message through his half moon glasses. "And who decided to put these men on the ship in the first place?"

"Joint decision. Ultimately sanctioned by the Secretary of State for Defence."

"Oh was it?" Thorpe would have things to say to David Carston at the morning's Cabinet meeting. "So he creates the problem and I am left to shovel up the dunghill," he protested.

"You describe this chemical they have got hold of as 'nasty'. Could you expand on that?"

"I can, Minister." It was Commander Taylor who replied. "I've been talking with Sir Graham Huish, Director of Lairig a' Mhuic. And I'm afraid it's about as nasty as it can get. It seems they've reduced the lethal dose to a single, complex molecular cluster, so the agent does not disperse. Hangs around indefinitely. And of course a tiny amount contains a phenomenal number of lethal doses."

"And they are threatening to release this in the London Underground?" Thorpe turned to Taylor's superior, the head of SO13. "Trevor? Situation analysis?"

"Bad. On three counts.

"One, we have to take them seriously. Anyone who can lift something from the strongroom of a frigate as sea is a force to be reckoned with.

"Two. If they go ahead the results would be appalling. The Tube is one big wind tunnel, and we know from tests that gasses are pumped around it at a phenomenal rate. It's only saving grace is that it disperses them equally quickly. That's the main reason Tokyo got away so comparatively lightly in March '95 when Aum Shinrikyo attacked their subway with Sarin. "But if this stuff doesn't disperse it would contaminate the entire network in a very short time if trains continued to run.

"And three, we are dealing with an unknown quantity as far as the PFLPE is concerned. We know they have some tie-in with the Battalions of Gaia, and they have claimed responsibility for four or five bomb attacks, but otherwise we know very little about them.

"It's always the same when you are dealing with wildcat extremist groups. You don't know what they are really after or how far they will go."

Thorpe looked unimpressed. "If they have been letting off bombs should you not have put somebody onto them?"

"I did. They killed him."

"I see."

"It was he who told us about the link with the Battalions of Gaia." Peacock explained the circumstances in which Neil Lamb had died. "He also gave us what we think is a name, but so far we have not been able to decipher it."

Thorpe then turned to the Director General of MI5.

"Geoffrey. Do you have anything to add?"

"Nothing I'm afraid. It's been in Trevor's court up till now. Obviously we shall now become involved. Mr. Tierney," he indicated his colleague, "will be handling it personally."

"Well I hardly need to say that we cannot close down the London Underground for a week. What other suggestions do you have?"

There was an uncomfortable silence, which Thorpe interpreted as the reticence that was invariably in evidence when a security operation had massive resource implications.

"I do realise this will be expensive," he prompted.

"It's not a matter of money, Neville," Sir Trevor Peacock said solemnly. "We could flood the Underground with every man and woman we've got, add all Geoffrey's resources and throw in the armed forces for good measure, and it still wouldn't help. We're not looking for someone with a bomb or a gun. All they need is to drop a few microscopic capsules where they will get trodden on, and the first we would know would be when people started dropping like flies."

"You are not suggesting that we do close the entire system down for a week?"

"I see little alternative, in the circumstances."

"It is unthinkable. The whole of London would grind to a halt. And we would be a laughing stock, not to mention the fact that we would be giving in to terrorism. Which as you know is directly contrary to government policy.

"No. It is quite out of the question."

Astutely Peacock gave him a few moments for the implications to sink in.

"Unfortunately, Neville," he said at last, "the alternatives are equally unthinkable. There could be untold numbers of deaths, and if it got out subsequently that we had been warned...."

He did not need to finish the sentence.

"But it would be giving in to terrorism," Thorpe repeated.

"No more so than evacuating a building when there is a bomb alert."

"It is not like you to take something like this lying down, Trevor."

"I am not lying down, and I don't like being pushed around by these slimeballs any more than you do, but I am simply facing facts. We will be working night and day, and following every lead possible, but at this moment we have no way of countering the threat, and 'within a week' starts now. Neither you nor I will survive if we allow an avoidable massacre."

The fact that he was referring to political survival rather than life itself did nothing to diminish the threat in Thorpe's mind. To him, as Peacock well knew, the two things were more or less synonymous.

"What concerns me," Geoffrey Bagnall put in, "is that if we do close the Tube for a week there is nothing to stop them simply waiting till it opens again. Or launching their attack elsewhere."

"Exactly," Thorpe agreed.

"If we publicly remove the marines from the *Lysander*," Peacock replied in measured tones, "and shut the Tube for seven days, there is a good chance they will feel they have had their pound of flesh."

"Okay. And then what?" Rear Admiral Owens saw the ball heading rapidly back in his direction. "We are back to square one. They still have us by the short and curlies, and if we've given in to blackmail once, what are they going to demand next time?"

"I don't know, Admiral, but we can only deal with one threat at a time. And that state of affairs would still apply if we called their bluff.

They could slaughter hundreds - thousands - of people on the Underground, and leave it contaminated and unusable for an indefinite period, and still have us by the 'short and curlies' as you put it."

"So we just give in? Throw up our hands and give them anything they ask for."

"No of course not. We catch them, and with any luck they'll be shot resisting arrest. But in the meantime do you have a better idea?"

"Yes. Refuse to close the Underground - if there is a chemical incident that is their responsibility, not ours - but appear to remove the men from the *Lysander*."

"What do you mean by 'appear to'?" Thorpe asked him.

"We take off five sailors instead. Out of a crew of two hundred and fifty there must be five who look sufficiently like the marines. No-one will know the difference. That way we still have our trump card in place."

The Home Secretary turned questioningly towards the head of the anti-terrorist branch.

"No," Peacock said firmly. "We don't know how the PFLPE found out about the marines, but it is more than likely they have someone on board the ship. If that is the case the substitution would almost certainly be spotted. We're in a deep enough hole already, and for the sake of keeping five men on a ship which by your own admission," he was now addressing Owens, "already has a compliment of two hundred and fifty, it is not worth the risk."

"These men have very special skills." It was Maj Gen Hugo Browne's first contribution to the discussion. "If anyone comes near that ship they will sort them out. That I promise."

"No. I agree with Sir Trevor," Thorpe said reluctantly but firmly. He was a decisive man when he needed to be, and much as he would like to find an alternative to what was being proposed he was tempted to point out that it was the Navy's decision to put the men aboard that had created the problem in the first place. "The SBS must come off.

"But," he said, addressing the anti-terrorist expert, "what about the idea of removing them, but not closing the Underground. Might that in itself be enough?" He knew he was clutching at straws.

Peacock shook his head. "Of course it's your decision, Neville, or rather the PM's. But I couldn't recommend that. As I said, when you are dealing with these small, maverick groups you have no idea what they may or may not do.

"If they have their hands on something as dangerous as Cdr. Taylor describes, this has to be handled with kid gloves."

Thorpe stared at him ungraciously.

"This is not going to go down well at No. 10," he said, sounding as if it might be Peacock's fault in some way.

"At least it will be a Cabinet decision. You can always fall back on the "collective responsibility" defence if the media give you a hard time," Peacock suggested.

But Thorpe's mind was already four hours ahead, when he would be explaining to the PM and the rest of the cabinet that he wanted to paralyse London for a week just two months before a General Election.

"It is not the media I was thinking about," he said stuffily, shuffling his papers into an orderly pile.

. . .

"Why do you do it?"

Jonathan Howarth peered quizzically at the rook he had just moved.

"Because you are challenging my queen."

"No," Hannah said reprovingly, wondering whether he had misunderstood on purpose. "Why do you kidnap people and hold them prisoner?" It was a question which troubled her considerably.

He laughed. It was meant to be a light-hearted chortle, but it did not work. It rang hollow - false and embarrassed.

"I don't exactly make a habit of it. As a matter of fact you are the first." He paused, and looked her in the eye. It required some effort. "And I am not enjoying it, Hannah. I enjoy your company, but I don't like keeping you here against your will."

"I know that. So why don't you let me go?"

"There is just too much at stake. I am committed to something I passionately believe in; something which overrides the convenience of individuals. Even you, I'm afraid."

144

"And it involves Rory?"

"In a way, yes. But as I've told you, he is a small part in the scheme of things, and there is no reason for him to come to any harm."

"So why won't you tell me what it is that is so important?"

He considered his answer carefully.

"Am I right in thinking that you are a member of the Battalions of Gaia?"

"Yes."

"So you are aware of the problems the world faces. There is not much disagreement about what they are, but there are three basic approaches to them.

"Firstly there are the flat-earthers and the head-in-the-sand brigade, who argue that global warming isn't a problem because a new ice age will balance it out, and as for all the other problems, new technologies will come along and magic them all away.

"Obviously you don't believe this any more than I do, or you wouldn't be a Bogger. It is wishful thinking developed into an art form.

"The middle ground is held by the majority view, which acknowledges the need for action, but believe it can be contained within the existing framework. Hold a few political summits, ban one or two chemicals, reduce carbon dioxide output by a few percentage points and stick brightly coloured recycling bins on street corners, and everyone feels they are doing their bit. It's all PR. It doesn't begin to address the problems. In fact some re-cycling does more harm than good.

"As far as I'm concerned this sort of tinkering around just distracts people's attention from the real scale and immediacy of the problem. I'm not sure whether this is a deliberate political ploy, or whether the politicians are simply too thick, or too busy pursuing their own self-interests, to grasp what's going on. It's probably a bit of both, but either way there is no political solution. Politics is the art of the possible, and there is no way you are going to get any electorate to vote for the sort of massive changes that are needed. Wholesale restructuring of society along environmentally sustainable lines.

"So the only solution - the third option - is direct action. Which is what we are taking. And I am afraid that you have just got caught up in it. I can't tell you what it is, or how you fit in, but I can assure you I wouldn't be holding you here if I did not believe it was a very necessary evil."

"That's exactly the sort of thing Dr. Flynn was saying at our last BoG meeting," Hannah said thoughtfully. How long ago was that? Four days? Five? It seemed like a lifetime.

"I'm pleased to hear that, but I don't think even the Battalions of Gaia are fully prepared, yet, for the sort of changes we propose."

"Like what?"

He smiled. "I can't tell you that just now. Suffice it to say that if we are successful you will hear about it very soon.

"Now," he said briskly, deliberately changing the tone and subject of the conversation, "would you like something to eat?"

"We haven't finished the game."

"Actually we have. You are mate in two moves." Hannah frowned at the board in front of her, trying to work that one out. "Would you like some eggs? They are free range. Or do you fancy something more solid?"

It was a strange internment, this. John, supposedly her gaoler, acted more like a butler. Or a friend even. During the day she was confined to her cell, but once dusk fell the main gates were shut and the three Dobermans were released into the grounds. John had shown her the dogs, and assured her, convincingly, that she would not make the garden wall alive. After that he gave her the freedom of the house at night, and because this was more agreeable than her cell she had started staying up later and later, and sleeping during the day.

John was good company, and had started to adjust his own hours to coincide with hers, often staying up with her half the night. He enjoyed board games, and also played table tennis and darts with her. He supplied her with almost anything she asked for, sending Carl out to the shops when necessary.

She could almost have enjoyed her incarceration were it not for worrying about Rory, and the disturbing presence of the revolting Carl, who slobbered about the place eyeing her in a way which made her skin creep. John seemed to have him under control, just, much as he did the dogs. But then they were not allowed inside the house. She had told John of her uneasiness, and he had taken the keys of her cell off the oaf, so at least she could sleep at night.

"How many eggs can you eat?" John called from the kitchen.

She went and joined him.

"Two please."

He broke them deftly into a bowl, beat them lightly with a few herbs, and dropped them into a pan in which a small coating of butter was just on the point of browning.

"Cheese?"

In response to her nod he added a small handful of crumbled Stilton, and a few chopped chives. Forty seconds later he turned out a perfect omelette.

"You start. Don't wait for me." He handed her the plate. "And it's just about time for the news."

Listening to the news on the World Service had become one of their nocturnal rituals. Tonight the main items concerned the Middle East, China and Paraguay, but for the third day running the bulletin included an account of the chaos in London caused by the closure of the Underground. In his precise, measured tones the announcer described the pandemonium that was being caused by the Government's decision to shut the network down 'for security reasons'. No explanation of this phrase had been offered, despite probing questions asked in the House, and various wild suggestions which had been mooted in the press. One of the tabloids favoured the theory that the tunnels had been found to be full of plague carrying rats.

Whatever the reason, the results were dire. On the first day the entire central area had ground to a complete halt, solid with traffic. Many commuters who set off for work never got out of their cars; some of them arriving home in the early hours of the following morning. Others, even less lucky, had to abandon their vehicles when they ran out of fuel or boiled dry, and these only added to the chaos.

After this fiasco the city was closed to private cars. Every available bus and coach in England, Scotland and Wales was then invited down to the capital to join in the hastily organised shuttle services; but provincial drivers did not know their way around the capital, and this measure was only a partial success.

147

Life in the City continued after a fashion. The British flair for coping in a crisis was much in evidence, and the most improbable figures could be seen wobbling to work on bicycles, their umbrellas strapped to the crossbar. Others simply did not go home, camping in the office till the situation sorted itself out.

But commerce was suffering, and some firms were not able to keep going. For some, on the margins, it might even prove to be the *coup de grâce*.

"What do you make of all that?" Hannah asked, as the report came to an end.

John wiped round his plate with a small piece of brown bread.

"I don't know," he said truthfully, though he had suspicions. He was not privy to the detailed plans of Richard Warrender and the others. Not because he was distrusted, or considered an outsider, but because each individual involved was told only what they needed to know in order to perform their duties.

For his part John knew about the Lairig connection, and he had, after all, sent Rory those knock-out drops. He knew what the Defence Research Establishment was all about, and it did not take an enormous leap of the imagination to see a possible connection.

Hannah watched him closely

"It hasn't got anything to do with my being here, has it?"

"I don't know, Hannah. I really don't."

"So you think it could?" she pressed.

"I can't say it is impossible. I am a foot soldier. Once you decide a cause is worth fighting for, and enlist, from then on you have to be prepared to take orders and do your bit. You can't expect the field marshals to fill you in on all the details of the overall battle plan."

She narrowed her eyes and her nose wrinkled. She peered at him, wondering how much of that was balderdash.

CHAPTER 9

If the passage through the Panama Canal had been uneventful the *Lysander* had not long cleared the western end before things began to happen. For want of other instructions Captain North had decided to continue on his charted course, but no more than half an hour after they had cleared Punta Mala a further signal was received from Northwood. The *Lysander* was to return to Balboa, where the stowaways were to disembark. After that it was to follow the coast North to San Diego.

Tom Bowen was fuming as he led his four men off the ship. This time it was a deliberately public affair, and the five of them left, dressed in borrowed clothes, down the main gangway.

As soon as they were gone the *Lysander* retraced her route out into the Pacific and, as instructed, turned north, up the west coast of America.

Captain North went on the main broadcast to inform the crew of this new itinerary, and again he invited Duncan up to the bridge to bring him up to date.

He began by explaining the arrival and departure of the SBS men, and then went on to speculate about the future.

"Needless to say a reception committee is being laid on for us in California - helicopters, mobile ops room, fast attack ships, Harriers, the works - but the terrorists," he spat the word out with the asperity of a man with three hundred lives in his hands and a gun at his head, "have demanded our fax number. They can contact us at any time. And I am under orders to follow their instructions to the letter."

Notwithstanding the distrust between the two men, Duncan could feel for North, having his command subverted and the prospect of receiving orders not from his appointed superiors in Northwood, but from a bunch of latter day pirates.

"The clever money," North continued, "says that we shall be stopped before we get anywhere near San Diego, and whatever these characters have in mind will occur when we are alone."

Confirmation of the accuracy of this prognosis came on the second day. The Guatemalan coastline had just given way to Mexico when the fax machine in the corner of the bridge began to print. An officer tore off the completed sheet and took it briskly over to where his Captain stood moodily staring ahead of him through the window.

North took the sheet of paper, cast his eyes over it, and blasphemed loudly. Seven surprised faces turned towards him in unison.

"This is it, Number Two. And it stinks." He passed the fax to his executive officer, his hand trembling with barely controlled rage.

As Ussher read the message the muscles of his jaw knotted, changing the contours of his five o'clock shadow. He looked at North, his senior by one stripe, his junior by eight years, and shook his head. "We've no choice, Christopher," he said firmly. "Would you like me to give the orders?"

"No. I shall do it." North turned to the other crew members on the bridge. "This message comes from the terrorists who boarded the ship and stole Mr. McLennan's nerve gas. It demands that we heave to, and that all crew members assemble on the foredeck. I must assume their intention is to board us." He looked at each individual in turn. "As you know our orders are to obey such instructions."

The faces around him showed that the implications of the entire crew assembled on the foredeck were well understood.

North addressed the helmsman. "Dead slow please, Barry. Steerage way only." Then he lifted the microphone from the console in front of him. "Now hear this," he said firmly. "This is the Captain. I have reason to suspect that we are about to be boarded. If I am right, these are the same men who assaulted able seaman Frost in the course of stealing material from the ship's arsenal. I do not know what more they want from us, but I am advised by the Admiralty that failure to comply with their demands will result in a large number of civilian casualties. It is for this reason that I am ordering all hands to comply with the following. I quote: 'To the Captain of the *Lysander*. You will stop your ship immediately. Everyone aboard is to assemble on the foredeck, with the exception of yourself, one senior officer, and your civilian passengers. These will be on the bridge. You know the consequences of failure to cooperate.' It is signed 'The Popular Front for the Liberation of Planet Earth', and includes a code phrase which authenticates the authors.

"I have no reason to doubt that they would carry out their threat, and therefore I want no heroics, and no-one is to act without specific orders." He paused. "Go to it then, and good luck."

He replaced the microphone and looked heavily round the bridge. "Mungo, you will stay with me," he told his executive officer. "To the rest of you I can only say I hope this damnable business will be over very soon." He saluted the five officers from the bridge as they filed out to join the human stream that was making its way for'ard.

Ussher by this time had a powerful pair of binoculars to his eyes and was scanning the horizon. "You'd think we should be able to see them," he said. It seems they know where we are. Is there anything on radar?" he called over his shoulder, momentarily forgetting that the navigation officer had just left the bridge. North walked over and checked the screen.

"Yes. Coming in on a bearing of one three zero." He watched for a few moments. "Height about three hundred feet, speed a hundred knots."

"Got it," Ussher answered from the port wing of the bridge. "Medium size chopper by the look of it."

The bridge was refilling with the civilians, and Duncan, Rory, Kingsley, and Goodyear followed North over to where Ussher stood. The speck in the sky was now visible with the naked eye, and growing by the minute into the recognisable shape of a helicopter. Within three minutes it was descending and slowing as it passed over the ship, and came to a halt hanging menacingly in the air a few cables' lengths ahead. The watchers on the bridge could see the occupants training glasses on the foredeck, satisfying themselves that their orders had been carried out.

The large, hovering creature then swung round and slowly began a tour of the ship, turning and dipping as it examined every inch of deck and peered into every crevice in the superstructure. Finally, infinitely slowly, it positioned itself to look directly into the windows of the bridge. Even without glasses Rory could see the faces of the occupants; those with binoculars could see the whites of their eyes.

"Pilot and six passengers," Ussher announced as the machine edged its way sideways, over the huddled ship's company, covering their ears and crouching in the fierce downdraught from the

151

helicopter's blades. Finally it swung round once again towards the stern, where it dropped lightly onto the flight deck. As it touched down four men leapt from the rear doors, machine guns at the ready. Two of them ran for'ard, and took up positions overlooking the foredeck, training their weapons on the men and women beneath. The other two remained as escorts to the two unarmed men who were the last to leave the machine. They were dressed in the same dark blue overalls as their watchful colleagues, and stooping beneath the slowing rotor blades, they in turn joined the two at the handrail below the bridge, where, for a long time, they looked down at the crowd below. Not long enough to count every head, but long enough to show they were taking nothing for granted. Finally, apparently satisfied, they made their way aft, flanked by the two machine gunners.

On the bridge Miles Roper had joined the others, panting either from anxiety or the exertion of climbing the companionways or both, and sucking noisily at his empty pipe he sounded like some ancient, wheezing traction engine. Ussher noted his arrival. "Are we all here now?"

Duncan made a quick check. "No," he said. "Damn. M.M. isn't here."

"What's his name?"

"Dr. Wilson."

North snatched up the microphone. "Dr. Wilson to the bridge at the double. Repeat, at the double." As an afterthought he offered the mike to Duncan.

"Charlie, this is Duncan," he said into it urgently. "It is essential that you get yourself up here immediately. You have about ninety seconds at most." He handed back the instrument and gave a shrug. "It's too late to go looking for him. We'll just have to hope he gets a move on." He looked out of the aft facing window. "I may have given him too long. They're heading up here now."

Wilson was still absent when the four men in overalls marched into the command centre of the ship, machine guns first.

"I gather there is someone missing," was Richard Warrender's opening remark.

"Yes," North replied tersely. "One of the scientists has not arrived yet."

"That is not a good start."

"You heard the broadcast. We've done everything possible."

"He's not a young man," Duncan added. "He may be asleep."

Rory was considering whether he had heard this man's voice before. He was certainly not The Voice, but could he have been the other? He was just reaching the conclusion that he was almost certainly not when a dishevelled figure appeared in the doorway, sleepily rubbing his eyes. "I hope this is important," M.M. muttered disgruntledly. Apparently oblivious of the presence of two men with machine guns, he blundered myopically towards Duncan demanding to know why his siesta had been disturbed. He had taken only two steps when one of the gunmen stepped in front of him, his weapon levelled at M.M.'s navel.

Wilson looked down at the gun and frowned. Then at its owner, and scowled. With a cursory flap of his hand he knocked the barrel aside and then grabbed the man by the lapels and began to shake him.

"I do not like being woken up," he growled, "and I certainly don't like having guns pointed at me."

The startled gunman let go of his weapon, which swung on its shoulder strap, and laid hands on his assailant. For a few seconds the two men grappled with each other till the unequal contest was ended with the younger, fitter man sending Charlie Wilson sprawling to the floor.

Winded, and in obvious pain, he crawled over to where Rory stood, and clung unsteadily to his young friend as he was helped to his feet.

"I shall overlook that incident," Warrender said magnanimously, "but any further such outbursts will not be tolerated." He then ordered everybody over to the starboard side of the room, where they and the entrances could be most easily covered by the two gunmen.

"I do not intend to make a melodrama out of this," he continued, when his captives were arranged to his satisfaction. "I am sure you know who we are and what we want."

Captain North raised his eyebrows. "As a matter of fact, I do not. If you are whom I assume you to be, you already have what you were after. I cannot imagine what more we have that could interest you."

"Ah yes, of course." There was the trace of a smile on Warrender's face, but he offered no further explanation as he turned to Ussher. "Who are you?"

"Commander Ussher. I am the ship's second officer."

"Right. You will escort my colleague here," he indicated the silent and watchful Toshihiko Yamamoto. "He will tell you where he wants to go. I am sure I need not go into details about what will happen if you do not do exactly as he asks."

"No." Many men would have wilted beneath the weight of invective which Ussher managed to instil into that word.

The two men left the bridge, and a hostile silence descended. It did not affect Warrender, however, who seemed to be amused by some inner thought.

"I don't know what you're up to," North said eventually, clearly irritated by Warrender's private amusement, "but you won't get away with it."

"Won't I? You surprise me Captain. Especially when you yourself have been of so much help. You really have been most cooperative."

"I have had no choice."

"You think not?" Warrender appeared to enjoy some private joke, his smirk becoming even more pronounced. "I am not so sure.I fear you may come to decide that you have not been quite as clever as you think you are."

North grunted. He was not going to allow himself to be baited, but he was determined to extract as much information as possible from his smug and loquacious captor.

"One thing I do know: you didn't do this without inside help. And I know too it is someone in this room." He watched the other's face for a reaction.

Warrender smiled, and then very slowly and deliberately looked at each of the faces opposite him in turn, missing no-one, and giving each the same, measured stare.

When it came to his turn Rory gritted his teeth and stonily returned the gaze. Would Warrender expose him? Probably not. He had not done anything yet. He was still an ace up this man's sleeve.

Except that they were all at his bidding now. The game was over, and he had won. He might no longer feel the need of Rory's support.

154

Warrender's eyes appeared to be boring into his soul, but after what felt like an eternity they moved on and eventually returned to settle back on North.

"Yes," he said evenly. "The entire operation was possible only because of one man."

"And yet you hold a gun on him," North taunted.

Warrender chuckled, and was working on a suitable riposte when Ussher and Toshihiko returned, each carrying two TCR's.

"Surprising what you find in paint stores, isn't it?" Warrender commented as they placed them on the chart table.

Ussher looked at him and shook his head. "I've already told your oppo here, these are dummies."

"That' right," Duncan confirmed. "They just contain water. I filled them myself."

Warrender raised an enigmatic eyebrow, walked over to the table, and unscrewed the top of the first canister. He drew out the glass phial from it's padded interior, and held it up to the light. It was half full of a clear liquid.

He repeated the exercise with the second one, with the same result. "As you say, it looks like water, but then how can one tell?"

"If you give it to me I'll drink it if you like," Duncan offered.

Warrender placed it on the table beside the first, and began to open the third TCR. This time, however, the phial he drew out and held up for all to see contained something entirely different. In this one a bright, coruscating, slightly viscous liquid, as green as a Martian's tears, clung to the side of the container as Warrender swirled it gently round and round.

No one person made a uniquely audible sound, but the combined, unconscious intake of breath created a collective gasp which rose above the background noises of the ship.

"Are you volunteering to drink this one, Mr. McLennan?" Warrender asked.

"I am not," Duncan said slowly.

"This does not altogether surprise me. But thank you for confirming its identity. He swilled the oily green solution once more round the glass, watching the light reflecting and refracting through it as it circulated. "It's an interesting feeling. Tosh," he said to his colleague. "Holding almost unlimited power in your hand."

Rory, like the others in the room, could not take his eyes off the phial. It was mesmeric: repulsive, yet at the same time enthralling. The only time he could recall such a sensation of skin-crawling enrapture was his first close encounter with the beautiful but deadly puff adder a friend of his had once kept.

So entranced was he that he was unaware that at his elbow M.M. seemed to be in some distress. He was making very little noise, but was in the throes of a coughing fit, quietly trying to suppress his spluttering by banging on his chest. So vigorous was this thumping that twice he struck Rory on the out stroke. The first blow brought him out of his reverie, the second gave him a strange sensation over his heart. Rory put his hand to his mouth, politely stifling a cough of his own, and lowered it, running it down the front of his jacket. It was a natural movement which caused no concern to the two gunmen at the other end of the bridge, their automatic weapons trained on the captives. But it brought Rory up with a start.

Because as his hand crossed over his heart he felt the unmistakable shape of a gun.

At his side M.M. had made a complete recovery, and was standing silent and composed, taking a great interest in the proceedings before him.

Rory suppressed the urge to laugh resonantly, and clap his old friend on the back. All that strange, and risky, performance with the guard when he first came in - he had been picking the man's pockets! And when he clung so clumsily onto Rory in his struggle to get up he had transferred it into his inside pocket. For a moment Rory's spirits soared. Thanks to the Great Mister Mysterio they now had a chance. A small one, to be sure, but a chance. They had a weapon and they had the element of surprise, as long as the guard did not discover the theft before their opportunity came.

But his spontaneous excitement condensed into a very cold mist when he thought of Hannah, and the possible implications of using the gun against the intruders. Unaware that he was doing so he bit his lip, and a thin trickle of blood began running down his chin as he forced himself to re-focus on the man before him, still savouring the feel of the phial he held triumphantly in his hand.

"I said that you might come to realise you are not as clever as you thought you were, Captain. I shall leave you to draw your own conclusions." Warrender was milking his moment of glory to the full.

"Our skin-diving companions could have taken it away with them," he continued, "but a three mile underwater swim in the dark, with half the world out looking for you, is a somewhat dicey undertaking. How much safer to have you bring it to us in your nice big boat. And of course it had the advantage that if your frantic searchers had found our swimmers, they would have had nothing incriminating on them.

"At the risk of repeating myself, you really have been most cooperative, Captain North. Most cooperative."

Warrender was goading North, and whether by accident or design was rubbing salt into his most open wound. One way or another he had been messed about and ordered around by civilians for the entire trip, and now he was being made to look a fool in front of his First Officer and passengers on his own bridge by a young whippersnapper of a terrorist. Christopher North was very close to his limits.

Rory watched Warrender's performance minutely, trying to gauge whether the goading had a purpose, or Warrender was simply indulging in an irresistible opportunity to crow. Meanwhile he was judging speed and distances, and calculating angles. He knew he had no choice. He could not imagine life without Hannah, but he was equally sure he could not live with himself if he did nothing now. And if he was going to act he did not have long. Once they began to withdraw it would be too late. Rory memorised the exact position of each person in the room, and where their attention lay. He deliberately slackened his muscles, and took a number of long, controlled breaths.

"All right," North was saying to Warrender in a tight, controlled voice. "You have what you came for. I should be grateful if you would get off my ship and release my men. In view of what you have in your hand you need have no fear that we shall use our armaments against you.

"But before you go I should like to know one thing: who is the traitor who helped you?"

"Traitor?" Warrender considered the word. "That rather depends on whose side you are on, doesn't it. I would prefer to describe him as a hero. A man who has risked his career, his reputation - even his liberty - not for any personal gain but in the cause of saving the planet. Doubtless that is a concept you find amusing. I am sure you think of us as cranks. But then being out of step with the majority does not necessarily mean being wrong. Ask Galileo."

Warrender smiled self-deprecatingly. "But this is not the time or the place for polemics. Yes, we are leaving, and our hero is coming with us, so your curiosity need distress you no further." He turned towards the group of captives. "Okay, I think it's time we left D...."

He got no further. The word was bitten off as Rory pounced on him, gun in hand. By moving slightly to his left he had placed Warrender directly between himself and one gunman, and he moved too quickly for the other to react. As his right hand rammed the barrel of the pistol into Warrender's cheek his left wrenched the phial from his grasp.

"Tell your men to drop their guns," he growled. "One, two, three...."

Warrender twisted round to face him, his eyes rounded to vicious circles.

"What do you think you're doing?" he hissed malevolently, his dilated pupils eating like acid into Rory's. "Give me that gun."

"Forget it."

"You do realise I have left instructions that if I don't return she is to die a particularly slow and painful death. And you are to be sent the video."

Rory faltered for only a moment, and then, his hand trembling dangerously, pressed the gun even harder against Warrender's skull. "Four, five, six...."

Warrender did not tell his henchmen to drop their weapons: Tosh had already done so. Dying an honourable death for the Cause was one thing. Watching his friend throw his life away pointlessly was another, and he had no doubt that Rory was more than ready to pull the trigger. And besides, they still had the upper hand overall, with the entire crew at their disposal.

As the two guns hit the the deck Duncan stepped forward to Rory's side.

"I don't know where you produced that gun from, laddie, but you've certainly pulled a blinder." He clapped him lightly on the shoulder, careful not to upset his trigger finger. "Here, let me help." He put out his hand and took the phial, swilling the green liquid round in its container. "Am I glad to see this again?" he said warmly. "I have to admit I had my doubts."

He turned back to the hero of the hour. "Your hand's shaking, Rory. Better give me the gun before you blow the poor wee chappie's head off." He stretched out his hand, and Rory gratefully handed over the pistol. He was not aware that he was shaking, but he knew he was very close to committing murder. The only thing stopping him at that moment was the knowledge that this man knew where Hannah was, and for that reason alone he wanted him to live.

And Rory was overwhelmed by a need to explain to Duncan, if he hadn't already guessed from Warrender's threat.

"Duncan, they've got Han...." As he turned to his boss he found himself looking down the barrel of the gun he had just relinquished.

"What the hell?"

Rory was not the only one present to react to this change of circumstances. Captain North, faced now with the identity of the viper that had been in the bosom of his ship for the last three weeks, stepped forward. Two rapid firing automatics at the far end of the room, capable of cutting the entire assembled company in half in less time than it would take to say 'Kalashnikov', had kept him in check, but one man with a mere handgun only a step away.... That was quite a different prospect. As he moved his fist began to swing towards Duncan's jaw, and Duncan in turn pirouetted round, gun first, to meet the attack.

Whether the fist or bullet would have landed first would have been decided in fractions of a microsecond, and it was even money as to which it would be. But in the event the contest was halted by the intervention, once again, of Charlie Wilson, who bounded forward and caught the Captain's fist as it began its forward trajectory.

"I wouldn't do that, me old mate. Not if I was you. Those bottles are supposed to be unbreakable," he indicated the phial in Duncan's hand, "but this wouldn't be a good time to put it to the test. If that green stuff got out it wouldn't do any of us any good."

"That's right, Charlie," Duncan agreed as he watched North biting back his rage. "And unbreakable is not the same as bullet proof." He shifted the barrel of the pistol from North's head, and pressed it against the bottle, holding both up for all to see.

"Why, Duncan?" Rory asked him, his voice almost breaking under the strained mixture of fury, incredulity and disgust. "For pity's sake, why?"

"Yes. I'd like to know that too," North growled, his even, pleasant features contorted into a mask of pure repugnance.

"Then perhaps, Captain, you should have read those leaflets you found in my room," Duncan replied. "Do you really believe we can continue to ignore the mountain of evidence that we are catastrophically and irreversibly turning the Earth into an uninhabitable rubbish dump? Oh I know we've bumped along so far, always finding some new technological fix to solve the problems created by our so-called progress. But we've reached the end. The problems have spiralled out of control. There are no quick fixes for overpopulation, global warming, atmospheric degeneration, desertification, rising sea levels.... If we are to do anything at all it has to be now, and it has to be drastic. And it will hurt.

"And since there is not a politician alive, in any country, who can stand up to the combined might of the power, oil and transport industries, it will have to be someone independent. Someone with courage, foresight, determination and power.

"And this," he said, shaking the bottle in his hand, "is the power source. With this the Popular Front for the Liberation of Planet Earth will be able, hopefully, to force the world to come to its senses, and make a serious and concerted attempt to save the planet."

As he finished his speech the sound of his voice was replaced by that of a slow handclap from Richard Warrender.

"There is more joy in heaven over a sinner that repenteth..." he quoted. "How gratifying to have a convert in our midst." He put out his hand. "If you are truly one of us, would you care to return those to me?" He indicated the bottle and the pistol.

"On one condition."

160

"Which is?"

"You take me with you. You can see I'm finished here, and I could be useful to you."

Warrender considered. There was no reason not to. It might help them get safely off the ship, and he could always be dumped in the sea if needs be.

"Why not? There's room in the chopper." He turned to Tosh. "Is that all right with you?"

"The more the merrier."

"Okay then." Warrender raised his eyebrows at Duncan, who nodded and handed the two items back to him.

Warrender did not point the gun at Duncan, but then he did not point it away from him either. He gave him a long, thoughtful stare.

"Before you go," Laurence Kingsley said firmly, breaking the sudden silence, "tell me your name."

Warrender raised his eyebrows. "What is it to you?"

Kingsley stood his ground. "Just tell me."

Richard stared at him, as unblinking and motionless as a reptile. He was thinking of the leaving present they had brought with them, which had taken up so much room on the helicopter. These men would be dead in a few minutes.

"Richard Warrender," he said, a note of pride in his voice. "A name I suspect you will remember till the day you die."

Kingsley took a slip of paper from his pocket and unfolded it. It bore the legend:

2 MEN, AUTOMATIC RIFLES, GRENADES,
.I(C/D).?A.(D/C).A..E(F/N)(D/C)E. BATTALIONS OF GAIA

He began fitting in the missing letters: R.I.C.H.A... "Oh yes, Mr. Warrender," he said, almost inaudibly. "I will remember you until I die."

Meanwhile Warrender turned to his companion. "C'mon Tosh. It's time we went." Toshihiko nodded his agreement, and Warrender turned back to the captives.

"Dr. Goodyear. If you are ready?"

Anthony Goodyear nodded, and walked across to him. There he turned towards his stunned colleagues, though he did not look directly at them. "I take no pleasure in this," he said, addressing no-one in particular. "I shall miss you as friends, and my work, and the others at Lairig. I hope you will believe that what I have done was not for personal gain - indeed I shall lose more than I could ever hope to gain by it. But I believe this to be right. To be necessary. No, not necessary, essential. As you see Duncan has reached the same conclusion. I hope the rest of you may do so too, before it is too late."

With no further farewell he turned and left the bridge. Tosh followed him, and Richard Warrender deferred to Duncan, inviting him to follow on. The two gunmen, their arms recovered, prepared to escort them out.

But Duncan hesitated. "Actually," he said uncertainly, "I think I might stay here after all."

Warrender looked at him suspiciously and raised the pistol. "What are you playing at, McLennan?" he asked dangerously.

"Nothing. It's just that I have a fear of flying," Duncan said innocently.

Warrender stepped forward and pressed the gun firmly into his stomach. "You are coming with us," he growled, "whether you like it or not. Now get moving."

Duncan did indeed get moving. In one smooth, swift movement he spun round through a hundred and eighty degrees, twisting the gun harmlessly off to one side, doubled up till his hands were on the floor, and lashed back with his right foot, his heel accurately aimed at Warrender's groin. The foot connected with a force which lifted Warrender off his feet and propelled him backwards several feet. The gun in his right hand went off, shattering a dial on the sonar display, and the glass phial in his left hand flew through the air over the heads of Wilson and Roper. Rory tore between them, flinging them apart, and dived at the falling bottle. In a save that would have made him Man of the Match in any cricket test he got his hand under it just four inches from the floor, and completed a rolling catch, holding the phial above his head as he came to a painful halt against the steel wall of the room.

In the meantime Richard Warrender had careered backwards into Laurence Kingsley, sending them both crashing to the floor, Warrender on top, Kingsley spreadeagled beneath him.

The gun landed at the feet of Duncan McLennan.

But Duncan made no attempt to pick it up. Rory, in the act of picking himself up at the other side of the room, assumed at first that he had not noticed the weapon lying in front of him, but then he caught sight of the two gunmen, moving in towards Duncan, their guns both levelled on him. To make a move for the pistol would be suicidal.

Duncan raised his hands theatrically above his head, and began to walk purposefully towards Miles Roper, speaking to him loudly in Latin. *"Nunc tamen interea haec prisco quae more parentum. Tradita sunt tristi munere ad inferias. Atque in perpetuum, frater, ave atque vale."*

It did not take a genius to realise that Duncan was up to something, but the problem for the gunmen was to know what. For a moment they hesitated, trying to read in his face some meaning to the cryptic message he was passing to his intellectual colleague.

But the message was not in the face; it was in the feet. Too late they realised it was not in the Latin verse, nor in Miles Roper, that the danger lay. As Duncan took his first step his foot sent the pistol sliding across the floor into the outstretched hand of Laurence Kingsley, and his subsequent walk towards Miles Roper cleared the line of fire between Kingsley and the gunmen. By the time the faster of the two had realised what was happening Kingsley already had the pistol in his hand. Instinctively the gunman swung his weapon towards the prostrate Kingsley, but even if he had been fast enough he could not have fired without almost certainly killing Richard Warrender, whose body obscured at least eighty per cent of Kingsley's. Two loud cracks rang out across the bridge, and both gunmen slumped to the deck with a limp, crumpling motion which suggested they were dead before they hit it.

Barely had they come to rest before Captain North and his first officer were beside them, recovering their fallen weapons. The group in the passageway turned at the sound of the shots to find themselves looking down the business end of North's Kalashnikov.

"Back in here at the double," he barked with an authority which rendered the gun almost superfluous.

Back in charge of his bridge, if not the ship, North looked two inches taller. He turned to Tosh and barked "Down!" Slowly and watchfully, like a cornered animal, Yamamoto lowered himself to the floor, and lay on his back. North pointed his weapon directly at his right kneecap, and called across to Warrender, who was struggling to extricate himself from Kingsley and rise to his feet.

"You. Call your men off now, or your friend will never walk again."

All eyes turned to Warrender, and Ussher walked over to the main broadcast microphone and lifted it from its cradle.

"Here," he said, holding it out. "You can use this."

Warrender looked at Tosh, and at Captain North standing over him, and slowly crossed the bridge to where Ussher stood. "It's switched on," Ussher told him, covering it with his hand. "You just have to speak."

Warrender accepted it.

"To the heroes of the Popular Front for the Liberation of Planet Earth: if you hear a shot, or do not hear from me every two minutes, you are to empty your weapons into the hostages."

He turned to North. "Those guns fire over a hundred rounds a second. So it's one of us for a whole lot of yours." He smiled questioningly. "Over to you Captain. The ball's in your court."

North looked at Tosh lying impassively at his feet, and stepped off him. And then, hefting his gun decisively, he marched across the room and let himself out onto the port wing of the bridge. He aimed the gun at the backs of the gunmen below and shouted: "Drop your weapons, we have disarmed your...."

The two men swung round in unison, opening fire as they did so. It was only then that North realised that despite having the advantage of surprise and height he was unable to return their fire. Standing as they were, against the handrail, from his vantage point they were silhouetted against the ship's company, crowded on the deck below and beyond. Any shot that missed would go into them.

North dived back into the safety of the bridge, kicking the door shut behind him as a vicious fusillade of bullets whined and thudded and ricocheted around the spot where he had been standing.

Warrender greeted his return with a wry grin. "What now, Captain?"

North scowled back at him, while reviewing his options. The demonstration of the fire power of the two Kalashnikovs had done nothing to ease his mind about the safety of his crew.

"Okay. It's a stalemate. Against my better judgement, therefore, I will give you safe passage off the ship."

"With what we came for."

"Without what you came for."

"No deal."

"Then what do you propose?"

"I propose," Warrender said loudly and distinctly towards the open microphone, his voice echoing back from loudspeakers all around the ship, "firing one shot into your huddled crew every minute until you agree my terms."

North shook his head. "It won't do. I should immediately kill you and your colleague. The gunmen down there are just as vulnerable from here as my crew are to them."

"You would lose a lot of sailors."

"You would lose everything."

This time there was no clever repartee from Warrender, just a thoughtful silence. Meanwhile North looked out of the window, and called his second officer over, turning off the main broadcast as he did so.

"Mungo. How long would it take you to go through the ship and up to the foredeck hatch?" They both stared down at the same point on the starboard side of the deck on which the crew were standing. Hidden from view beneath the throng of people was an escape hatch for crew members working in the bows. "If you could pass this out," he indicated his Kalashnikov, "to one of the marines they could take those blighters out from below."

Ussher considered. "Not in two minutes."

"You haven't got two minutes," Warrender crowed, looking at his watch. "It's only eighty-five seconds now before I broadcast or my men start shooting. And of course I shall share your thoughts with them."

"With your permission, Captain." It was Laurence Kingsley who broke into North's frantic thinking. "Might I try something?"

"By all means."

165

Kingsley turned to Rory and put out his hand. "The bottle please."

Rory handed it to him. He did not know who or what he was, but Laurence Kingsley had proved himself in action.

Kingsley took it over to Warrender. "Here, he said, "this is what you want, isn't it? Well take it." Warrender held back suspiciously. Kingsley thrust the bottle into his hand, took hold of his other wrist, and twisted it up his back until he winced. Then, holding the pistol to the back of his neck, frog-marched him across the bridge and out of the door which North had used. He twisted his captive round to face the bows, keeping his own body directly behind him.

"Right," Kingsley growled. "If they shoot now they get you and your bottle of poison. And you get nothing except a lot of holes in you." He gave Warrender's arm and extra twist. "So tell them to drop their guns."

The pain which shot through his upper body brought tears to Warrender's eyes, and seemed to cloud his mind. But even as his brain swum it occurred to him that Kingsley was wrong. He would gain something by dying now. He would be a martyr for the cause. There would be more publicity, more discussion. It would be an event around which others would build, a rallying point for the faithful.

Except.

If the bottle went now in a hail of bullets it would create local pollution, but nothing on the scale he had planned. And as it would wipe out everybody on the ship the navy could, and would, create any story they liked around the incident. And it would not include an account of his own heroic self-sacrifice.

As a living martyr, however, he would be tried, and he could use his trial as a public platform. He could imagine the crowds of supporters outside the court, the television cameras, and the acres of newsprint that would travel across the world.

"Drop your guns," he shouted. "In the name of Gaia, drop your guns."

Kingsley waited until they had complied, and the marines had taken charge of them and the helicopter pilot, and then marched Warrender back inside.

"Thank you, Commander." North greeted him. "And well done."

"Commander?" Rory echoed. "You are a naval officer?"

Kingsley turned to him and smiled. "Not at all. Metropolitan Police. anti-terrorist section."

"So...." Rory turned towards Duncan, his mind racing to rearrange the jigsaw into a meaningful picture.

"That's right, laddie," Duncan confirmed. "My good friend Laurence here is on the side of the angels." He paused. "And so am I, in case you're still wondering."

Kingsley gave a little bow, and then turned to Duncan.

"I liked the quotation, by the way. 'But now meanwhile take these offerings....' if I remember my Latin correctly. Very apposite."

"So why did you give him the T2?" Rory asked Duncan, indicating Warrender.

"To flush out Dr. Goodyear. Until he had exposed himself I couldn't afford to have their pitch queered."

Rory flushed with anger. Not just because of what Duncan had put him through after he had risked his life to overcome Warrender, but for the recklessness of it. He shook his head in disbelief.

"I can't believe that anyone, let alone you, would take a risk like that with so many lives. You were prepared to hand the initiative back to them, even knowing what that bottle contains? "

Duncan smiled and shook his head gently. "Especially," he emphasised the word, "knowing what the bottle contains." As he spoke he took the phial from Kingsley and, as everyone watched, unscrewed the lid, took a small swallow, and pulled a face.

"Does anyone actually like crème de menthe?" he asked rhetorically, and answered himself: "I suppose Graham Huish must do. It was all I could find in his office. Now if it had been Laphroaig...." he said, addressing the green liquid wistfully.

Rory screwed up his eyes. "Is that what all this was about? A trap for Anthony?"

"To begin with, yes. I have known for some time that information was being leaked out of Lairig, some of which should only have been available to the section heads. But I didn't know which one. I dreamed up this trip as a way of flushing the guilty one out, with the fictional T2 as the bait. But in the process of negotiating with the powers that be I came across Commander Kingsley, and it occurred to us both that we might have hold of different ends of the same ball of string. He was investigating the connection between the so-called Popular Front for the Liberation of Planet Earth and the Battalions of Gaia, after his predecessor was murdered by them."

"So who killed Skinner and Dobbs?"

"I'll fill you in on that in a minute. Let's help sort out these four first." He indicated the two live and two dead intruders, and Anthony Goodyear.

"As soon as they've finished mopping up down below I'll get a medical detail to take the corpses away," North told him. "The other three will be locked up till we get home."

"There's something else." Rory did not look at anyone in particular. "They've got Hannah. They took her before we left. I was supposed to help them."

"Then what you did just now was even braver that I realised," Duncan said warmly.

"Indeed it was," North agreed. He looked round the room. "Would you leave us alone for a few minutes, please." He indicated Rory and Warrender as the ones to stay. "And Mungo, wait outside and see that no-one comes in."

Three marine officers were just arriving, and Yamamoto and Goodyear were placed in their custody and led away. Rory found himself alone on the bridge with Warrender and the Captain. North turned to his captive, pistol still in hand, and said: "There is a telephone here. I want you to get the girl released."

Warrender stared at him defiantly. "Then you can go on wanting."

The speed with which the pistol swept up and hit him on the side of the face took him totally by surprise. He had no time to ride the blow, and took it full force. A large red weal appeared immediately, and blood began to trickle down from his ear.

"Listen Mister," North growled. "You have invaded my ship, ordered me around, and threatened my crew. So why do you think I asked the others to leave? I don't much care what happens to you, but you have a choice: you get the girl released, or you die trying to escape. Which is it?" He picked up the telephone receiver and thrust it at the cowering man.

Warrender took the instrument and made the call. When Jonathan Howarth came on the line he said simply: "It's Richard. I want one of you to take the girl back where you found her."

EPILOGUE

Hannah shuddered, and drew herself closer to Rory.

"Do you really think he would have shot him in cold blood?"

Rory shrugged. "I don't think his blood was cold. As a matter of fact, I think it was pretty near boiling. But I don't know. I don't suppose he did.

"Anyway it didn't come to that, and it worked. You're back, and that's what matters as far as I'm concerned."

She stared thoughtfully at a mark on the carpet. "So the end justifies the means?"

"No. But the means and the end have to balance. The end must be worthy of the means." He gave her a little squeeze. "In this case it definitely was."

"It's ironic, isn't it. For me to be kidnapped by environmentalists, and freed by the Navy. I suppose it confirms all your prejudices?"

"What prejudices are those?"

"That environmentalists are left-wing trouble-making scaremongers."

"I've never said that. As a matter of fact I rather admire those men in a strange way. From their perspective they were quite right. They were fighting for something they believed in; not for personal gain. And they were prepared to put their lives on the line for it.

"I don't approve of their methods, but I can still respect them."

"Even though they were going to kill people?"

"Even though they were going to kill me, and everybody else on board the *Lysander*. There was a very large time bomb in their helicopter which they were going to leave behind in the armoury. It would have blown the ship apart.

"But from their point of view they were waging a war. And people get killed in war."

"But you say they didn't kill those two scientists?"

"No."

"So who did?"

He was silent for a moment.

"It was suicide, just as the papers said. They had been living together quite openly for years, and just as they were nearing the ends of distinguished careers some pea-brain in the MoD cottoned on and decided a homosexual relationship was a security threat. They were about to be dismissed. Dishonourable discharge. Couldn't face it."

"How awful." She thought a while. "So Duncan made up the story about them being killed because they'd invented that gas? Isn't that a bit tacky?"

"I thought so at first, but it's ends and means again. On reflection I think they would have been pleased that something positive came out of their deaths. That they had helped stop the leaks from Lairig.

"Mind you, I'm glad in a way they've been spared all this. They were good friends of Dr. Goodyear's. They'd have been devastated."

"Talking of being devastated," she asked, "did you ever find out why that other scientist - Dr. Roper - got so upset about having his cabin searched?"

"No. He obviously had something in there which he was ashamed or embarrassed about, but Captain North wasn't telling. He took the line that it had nothing to do with the matter in hand, so it should remain Miles' own business."

"And you've no idea?"

"Well women's underwear was mentioned, but that's only a rumour."

She twisted her head in his lap and looked up at him sideways. "You're quite friendly with him, aren't you? Do you think he's that type?"

He smiled. "It's like the terrorist thing. There is no 'type'. He's a nice bloke, and if that's what he gets off on it's up to him. It's harmless enough compared with many things I can think of."

She snuggled back into his lap, and he lay back and looked up at the picture over the fireplace.

" '...an air that kills from yon far country blows,'" he quoted from the stanza he had learned by heart. "That could have been very literally true. Thank heavens it didn't exist."

"But it does exist!" she cried, sitting up abruptly. "It's belching out of every car and every aeroplane and every factory and every power station in the world. The fact that Duncan's chemical was a hoax doesn't alter anything. The problem hasn't gone away you know."

"No, I know." He pulled her back to him, annoyed at himself. Their reunion had been going well up to now. "It hasn't made things any better, but it hasn't made them worse, either. You may even get some useful propaganda out of it.

"But you haven't told me how you were treated. You must have had an awful time."

"Well it wasn't exactly a load of fun, but it could have been worse. It was horrible to begin with; being kidnapped, and wondering what was going to happen. But after that, once I knew I was safe, the worst part was being cut off from everyone, and wondering what was happening to you."

"Being safe!" he said in genuine amazement. "You do know they threatened to chop you up and post me the pieces?"

She chuckled. "John! Cut me up? I don't see it somehow. He wouldn't hurt a fly."

"Is this the man who kept you locked up in a cellar?" he asked incredulously.

"He didn't want to. And he let me out at night. They had guard dogs in the garden then, so I couldn't run away, and he gave me the run of the place. In the end I was staying up most of the night and sleeping in the day, and he used to stay up and keep me company. We played chess and he cooked me meals. He was a super cook."

"You make it sound as though you enjoyed it."

"No, of course not. But the thought of him hurting me is ridiculous. He was a perfect gentlemen."

"He didn't try anything on then?"

"No, nothing like that. He just did everything he could to make my time there as easy as possible. And he protected me from the other man who I didn't like one bit. He made my skin crawl, and he did make lewd suggestions. It was him that phoned you up. I think John thought that if he rang you himself you wouldn't take him seriously."

"The Voice," Rory said. "So that's who it was. And when I rang back I suppose I spoke to this John character?"

"I only knew about the one phone call. But if you rang a portable it probably was John. He carried one all the time, though he didn't use it much when I was around. Apart from anything else it was mostly night time."

"He had a respectable, educated voice?"

"Yes. He used to be a research chemist for the Government, or something."

"Did he, begorra! No wonder he was able to get me the knock-out drops for Terry."

"How is Terry, by the way? Not very pleased with you, I suppose."

"He's being very good about it. Says he'd have done the same in my position. And he's fine. Apparently the stuff wore off very quickly."

"And Duncan?"

"Ah, yes. Duncan. Well Duncan is not the world's most popular man at the moment. He has always liked to play things close to his chest, and it seems that while he cleared the trip with Whitehall he failed to mention that the T2 was a put-up job. Of course he had no way of knowing where it would lead, but I gather HM Government are not overly amused at having shut the London Underground for a week on the strength of a bottle of crème de menthe!"

He must have had a hell of a nerve to keep it to himself in the circumstances," she said admiringly.

"He says he had no choice. That Westminster is too leaky, and if he'd told anyone it would have become common knowledge in no time. So only Sir Graham and Kingsley were in on the secret.

"Anyway, he's got away with it. By trapping the PFLPE, who had after all let off a number of bombs, not to mention murdering a policeman, he's too big a hero for them to do anything about it."

"And what about you?"

"Well Duncan is taking the line that I should have gone to him earlier, but I redeemed myself by sticking a gun up Warrender's nose at the crucial moment."

There was a pause. "How do you feel about that, by the way?" he asked at last.

"About what?"

"The fact that I risked your life rather than do what they wanted?"

She twisted onto her back and looked up at him. "You did what you knew was right. I wouldn't have wanted it any other way."

173

He smiled down at her upturned face. "I love you, Hannah Gentle."

"And I love you, Rory McLennan." She returned his smile. "I don't think I realised how much until I was kept away from you."

"It's an ill wind etcetera etcetera."

"Exactly." She screwed up her nose in the endearing way she had. "You don't fancy a move do you?"

"What sort of a move? Where to?"

"Anywhere. Just a place of our own."

"As a matter of fact,"he said, gently stroking her forehead., "as a matter of fact I was thinking something very much along those lines myself."